"We need to reach—" Beatrice never finished her sentence. The words ended in a gurgle as a hand clamped firmly over her mouth and dragged her back. Ah So let out a small cry and then she, too, was pulled toward the rear of the stage by a man dressed in a quilted cotton suit of the purest coal black.

Slocum never asked questions. He dived forward, tackling the Chinaman trying to abduct Beatrice. He found himself at the bottom of a pile of punching, kicking highbinders. One blow glanced off the side of his head, stunning him. Another smashed squarely into his temple. Everything went black . . .

JAKE LOGAN

SLOCUM AND THE FRISCO KILLERS

J

JOVE BOOKS, NEW YORK

SLOCUM AND THE FRISCO KILLERS

A Jove Book / published by arrangement with
the author

PRINTING HISTORY
Jove edition / November 1996

All rights reserved.
Copyright © 1996 by Jove Publications, Inc.
This book may not be reproduced in whole
or in part, by mimeograph or any other means,
without permission. For information address:
The Berkley Publishing Group, 200 Madison Avenue,
New York, New York 10016.

The Putnam Berkley World Wide Web site address is
http://www.berkley.com/berkley

ISBN: 0-515-11967-9

A JOVE BOOK®
Jove Books are published by The Berkley Publishing Group,
200 Madison Avenue, New York, New York 10016.
JOVE and the "J" design are trademarks
belonging to Jove Publications, Inc.

PRINTED IN THE UNITED STATES OF AMERICA

10 9 8 7 6 5 4 3 2 1

For John and the long and winding road.
Happy trails, old partner.

SLOCUM AND
THE FRISCO KILLERS

1

John Slocum gripped the rail tighter in anticipation of the starter's bell. He tried not to yell like the people in the crowd around him when the horses leaped from the gate and thundered past him. He clutched five one-hundred dollar tickets to win on Heavy Seas, the finest three-year-old thoroughbred Slocum had ever seen set a hoof on a racetrack. In the week he had been following the nags at Bay District Race Track outside San Francisco, Slocum had seen the horse win every race easily. Today, Heavy Seas looked to be in top form.

"Run or I'll sell you to the glue factory!" bellowed a florid man a few paces off to Slocum's right. As the well-dressed man turned to watch the horses round the second turn and race into the backstretch, Slocum had to squint. The sunlight caught the man's headlight diamond and almost blinded Slocum. It had to be a two-carat stone from the way it bounced so heavily on the man's gray silk cravat. Everything about the man spoke of money—lots of money. But it wasn't the obviously wealthy man who held Slocum's attention.

The young woman crowding close to the man was tall, slender, and had a flow of blonde hair that cascaded halfway down her back to tantalize her slim waist with every move she made. She turned and flashed Slocum a quick smile. His green eyes met hers for only an instant, but it was enough to leave him with a warm feeling. Such beauty was unexpected, no matter where he found it.

Finding it at the Bay District Race Track was even more of a surprise, though he knew rich men often brought their ladies to the afternoon races. The man on this woman's arm was obviously rich, but the couple was a complete mismatch. This woman could have any man she wanted, and there had to be others as rich as the portly gent so pointedly ignoring her while the horses ran. Slocum couldn't keep his eyes from drifting to the man's diamond stickpin, and he wondered how deep this motherlode of fortune ran. When a new cheer went up from the crowd, the florid man jerked free from the woman's grip and he began shouting.

"Don't flag on me, you miserable glue pot. Run, damn your brown eyes, *run*!"

The portly man meant Heavy Seas, the same horse Slocum had bet on so heavily. After spending the past week studying the horses, their trainers, and the jockeys, Slocum knew Heavy Seas was as close to a sure thing as they came. The other horses were clearly outclassed by the thoroughbred. The race went off at only five to three in favor of Heavy Seas, but Slocum had laid down five hundred dollars in spite of the poor potential return.

Heavy Seas wasn't going to lose.

"Run, put the whip to him, keep him running!" shouted the portly bettor. Although he completely ignored the blonde lady with him Slocum saw her attention was fixed on the race, also. She chewed on her lower lip and fluttered her fan nervously. He wondered how much they had bet on Heavy Seas.

"Look, on the outside. It's Lost King. Lost King is coming on strong."

Slocum blinked in astonishment. Lost King was a long

shot, a hundred-to-one horse and no match for Heavy Seas. But Lost King pulled even with Heavy Seas in the far turn and every stride put a few more inches of space between them. Heavy Seas clearly tired, lather flowing from the stallion's heaving flanks in frothy sheets. The more the jockey used his whip, the worse the horse fared. When Heavy Seas broke stride in the homestretch, Slocum knew he had lost five hundred dollars.

Lost King crossed the finish line a half dozen lengths ahead of Heavy Seas.

"No, this can't be," moaned the red-faced man, growing redder by the minute as his anger mounted. He leaned heavily against the rail, shaking his head and banging a pudgy fist on the rail as if he wanted it to be someone's face. "Heavy Seas couldn't have lost."

"But he did, Papa," the blonde said, her hand resting on his arm. The man jerked away angrily. "There's never a sure bet in horse racing. Haven't you told me that often enough?" Her words did not soothe him. If anything, they drove him to even greater fury.

"Heavy Seas couldn't have lost! I'll have that jockey's head on a platter!"

"You lose, too?" Slocum asked, holding up his sheaf of worthless tickets, before stuffing them into his side pocket. "That's a fine horse. Wonder what happened to him?"

"He's my horse," the man said, chest rising and falling heavily as he gasped for breath. "I'm going to sell it to the first man with two bits in his pocket."

Slocum started to speak, then clamped his mouth shut. No matter how this race had turned out, he would have bought Heavy Seas if the man was serious about selling, but every last dollar Slocum had to his name had been shoved across the narrow counter in the grandstands to buy the tickets. He had been that sure of winning.

The man turned even redder in the face and pushed past

Slocum, huffing and puffing as he stormed along the track in the direction of the stables.

"I'm sorry if he seems rude. This is so unexpected," the blonde said, smiling faintly in Slocum's direction. "My papa truly expected Heavy Seas to be an easy winner. He lost more than ten thousand dollars on this race."

"That's a heap of money," Slocum allowed. "I'm John Slocum." He tipped his hat in the woman's direction. Her emerald eyes danced.

"Allow me to apologize. All my manners have been forgotten owing to this small setback of our fortunes. I'm Beatrice Keller."

"That's Henry Keller?" Slocum thought he was past surprise, but he found he was not.

"You find that so outrageous?"

"Not at all. I've heard of Henry Keller ever since coming to San Francisco a couple months ago," Slocum said. "The man is well known in racing circles. He owns Heavy Seas?"

"And ten other fine horses," Beatrice said, "but none compares with that stallion. How Heavy Seas could have been beaten by a nag like Lost King is a true mystery." She pursed her bow-shaped lips, as if in deep thought on the matter. Slocum had never seen a more beautiful woman in all his born days.

"The money's no real concern to your father, is it?" asked Slocum.

"What he lost wagering? Oh, yes, it always is. Papa is very frugal and never likes to lose money. I have seen him fly into a perfect rage over being shortchanged at a restaurant."

"I've heard he's about the richest man in San Francisco."

"No, not at all," laughed Beatrice Keller. "Mr. Crocker and Mr. Sutro are far richer. And there is—"

Slocum hardly needed the recitation of San Francisco's richest railroad, mining, and banking magnates to know

Beatrice moved in high social circles. Far higher than he would ever inhabit, even if he had won with his bet on Heavy Seas.

"Oh, excuse me, Mr. Slocum. There's Papa's assistant, William Considine, waving to me. I must join the others in my party. How am I going to explain Heavy Seas' loss to them? I am sure they all bet as heavily as my father. He had been touting the stallion as a sure bet."

"There aren't any sure bets," Slocum said, sorry to see the woman leave.

She turned and glanced back over her shoulder at him, eyelashes batting coyly. "I hope it is a sure bet that we are going to see one another again, Mr. Slocum."

All he could do was shrug. With nothing but holes in his pockets, he wasn't likely ever to be anywhere their paths might cross.

"I work in a mission down in Portsmouth Square. The Portsmouth Square Rescue Society. Papa thinks I spend all my time and all his money on the poor Chinese émigrés. Do stop by sometime and tell me what you think." With that, she turned and hurried off to where her father's assistant stood glowering. The bulky man seized Beatrice's arm and roughly pulled her along. They exchanged words Slocum couldn't hear, but Beatrice was not pleased at what he said and Considine even less so by her reply.

Slocum's quick eyes picked up the bulge at Considine's side pocket. A few greenbacks poked out. If Keller had lost heavily at the track, Slocum guessed his hired hand had not. As if noting Slocum's attention, Considine shoved his hand into his pocket and pushed down a thick wad, then circled his arm familiarly around Beatrice Keller's waist. She chatted merrily, but the glare Considine gave Slocum might have frozen Eskimos with its cold intensity.

Slocum continued watching the couple until they melted into the crowd in the grandstands heading for the posh Jockey Club. All the way, Considine kept looking back at Slocum as if he intended to spin around and draw. The bulge in his side coat pocket might have been a wad of greenbacks thick enough to choke a cow, but the one under his left arm had to be a six-shooter slung in a special harness. And Slocum had seen enough gamblers in his day to know what the lump in the vest pocket meant. A derringer rode there. Considine might even carry a knife strapped around his thick middle.

Henry Keller's assistant was one dangerous cayuse.

Slocum turned and headed for the stables. He touched his own coat pocket and the worthless tickets there. He wouldn't have been rich if Heavy Seas had won, but he wouldn't be wondering where his next meal would come from, either. Slocum had to find out what had gone wrong in the backstretch. By the time Heavy Seas had come into the homestretch, the race was well nigh over.

Slocum passed Henry Keller, but the portly man gave no indication he saw anyone. He stormed away from the stables, heading for the Jockey Club and its liveried waiters and linen-clothed tables. If ever a man needed a drink, Slocum thought, it was Keller. For all that, Slocum could use a drop or two of whiskey to wet his whistle. It had been a long, discouraging day.

He stopped at the entrance to the paddock when a burly Chinese strutted past. The sight of such an arrogant Celestial aroused Slocum's curiosity. While it was not uncommon for Chinese to bet at the track, having one enter the stable area struck Slocum as peculiar. He trailed the swaggering man dressed in the too-small suit. Slocum's curiosity almost screamed when it became apparent that the Celestial was headed for the stall where Heavy Seas was getting a rubdown after the race.

The groom looked up, then stepped forward and spoke in hushed tones to the Chinaman. The hulk of a man laughed harshly and reached into his coat pocket, passing over a thick envelope. Slocum's hand drifted toward his six-shooter, then stopped. He had no idea what was going on—but he had strong suspicions. Before he could step forward and confront the Celestial and the groom, angry voices stopped him. Slocum faded into the shadows of an empty stall by the door.

Another Celestial entered, arguing with a trainer. This Chinaman was dressed as opulently as Henry Keller and showed the same easy haughtiness brought by fabulous wealth.

"I can't give nuthin' like that to my horse. It'd kill 'er for sure," the trainer complained. He looked around, fearful of being seen. Slocum moved deeper into shadow and listened hard.

"Your horse will win. What will be the odds?" the Celestial asked in a sibilant voice that both caressed and left Slocum feeling oily and degraded. He could only guess how the trainer reacted.

"Two hundred to one, maybe," the trainer said. "If I bet a lot, less."

"There will be little wagering on Irish Cloverleaf. *We* will become fabulously rich."

"You already are, Little Pete," the trainer said nervously. From the trainer's expression, Slocum knew the man wanted to join the Chinaman in the deposit line at the bank. The trainer heaved a deep sigh, coming to what had to be a foregone conclusion. "Thass the way I wanna be. Ol' man Proctor don't pay shit for the work I put in on his nags, the cheap son of a bitch."

"He will be surprised at your expertise," Little Pete went on, "if Irish Cloverleaf wins. You will be in great demand with other, better stables as a trainer."

"Yeah, could be," the trainer said. "Gimme. Give it to me so I can do it." The trainer took a small envelope from Little Pete and hurried off. Slocum remained hidden when the burly Celestial strutted up to the smaller Chinaman. They spoke rapidly in their singsong language, then left together. Slocum had no doubt who was the boss and who was the inferior. The huge man walked three paces behind Little Pete.

Slocum started to follow, but bumped into William Considine's broad chest. Slocum recoiled and stared up into the man's cold, dark eyes.

Considine reached out and grabbed Slocum by the lapels and lifted. The seams in Considine's coat threatened to split as he strained to keep Slocum up on tiptoe.

"You stay away from Miss Keller," Considine growled. He blinked when Slocum reached up and grabbed a thick wrist. Twisting hard, he pried Considine's fingers loose from his jacket.

"What concern is it of yours?" Slocum had no designs on the woman, but being threatened riled him. He didn't take this kind of harassment off any man.

"I'm gonna marry her, that's what," Considine said. "I work for her old man, and it's my job to protect them. *Both* of them."

"Is it your job to carry their money around?" Slocum's cold green eyes dropped to the side pocket that had bulged with money. To his chagrin, the pocket hung flat and empty. Considine had gotten rid of the greenbacks that had been stuffed there only a few minutes earlier when Slocum had seen him in the grandstand.

"What I do is keep no-accounts like you away from them. I'll break you in half if you bother them again, especially Miss Keller." Considine went to shove Slocum but missed as Slocum turned to the side and let the meaty hand slip past. He balled his fist and considered driving it into the obnoxious man's exposed belly, but he held back. He had no call to start a fight.

The bell rang and the horses leaped from the starting gate as the next race began. Considine glowered, saw he wasn't cowing Slocum, and made an obscene gesture as he turned and left. Slocum watched Keller's bodyguard— that was all a man like William Considine could ever be— and finally pushed the threat from his mind.

The warning from Considine added some fuel to a fire burning within Slocum, but it would have to go out on its own. Seeing Beatrice Keller again would be nice, but Slocum knew it wasn't going to happen. They moved in different social circles, and he would never have the chance of even getting close enough to tip his hat in her direction.

The noise of the crowd dwindled, then rose to an ear-splitting cacophony as the horses rounded the far turn and pounded into the homestretch. Slocum got to the rail in time to see a horse with green and white silks far ahead of any of the others. Slocum didn't need to be told the broken-down mare winning so easily was Irish Cloverleaf, and that the trainer had given the horse whatever Little Pete had passed over in the envelope.

"The Irish Cloverleaf pays one twenty-five to one," bellowed a steward walking through the crowd. "Collect your winnings, you lucky people. Next race in fifteen minutes!"

Slocum watched the crowd flow toward the grandstand, leaving Little Pete at the rail. The Celestial smiled broadly as he took a small notebook from his pocket and entered a notation.

"You doped that horse," Slocum said. "You drugged Heavy Seas, too, so he would lose. You're fixing races." As Slocum spoke, his cold anger turned white hot. He took a deep breath, settled his emotions, and stared at Little Pete. "Because of you rigging the races, I lost five hundred dollars."

"Some win, some lose, that is the way of the parimutuel," Little Pete said softly. He looked Slocum over from head to foot, then obviously dismissed him.

"I want the eight hundred I would have won if you hadn't doped Heavy Seas."

Little Pete let out a curt laugh, turned, and started to walk away without saying a word. Slocum grabbed and caught the man's shoulder, spinning him around. Little

Pete's expression had not changed, but Slocum felt as if the temperature at the Bay District Race Track had suddenly dropped twenty degrees.

"My money, or I turn you in to the track stewards," Slocum threatened.

The only warning he had was a large shadow moving on the ground. He ducked but still took a powerful blow on his shoulders, which knocked him down.

2

Heavy fists hammered at Slocum, driving him back to the ground every time he got his feet under him. He finally rolled onto his back and kicked hard, catching Little Pete's bodyguard in the belly. Slocum thought he had slammed his boots into a rock wall. The giant of a Chinaman grunted but otherwise showed no sign that the mule kick affected him.

Slocum kicked again at the man's kneecap, forced the Chinaman back, then rolled to the right and came to his feet. His hand flashed for the Colt Navy slung in his cross-draw holster, but the Celestial was quicker than his bulk suggested. He grabbed Slocum's wrist and twisted hard. Bones cracked and pain shot into Slocum's forearm as the pressure mounted. He had no choice but to release the ebony butt of his six-shooter. As he did so, he punched with his left hand, but the blow was awkward and bounced off the Celestial's cheek without doing any real damage.

"Lee Chuck! Stop it!" came the cry.

Slocum didn't turn to see who shouted. He was too busy trying to keep from dying. The Celestial released Slocum's wrist and clamped his powerful hand on his victim's exposed windpipe. Slocum felt the energy draining from him and the darkness closing in from all around. Try as he might, he could not pry loose the muscular hand choking him to death.

Then Slocum gasped, the pressure gone from his throat. He crashed back into the rail and spun around. Struggling to stay on his feet, he drew his six-gun.

"None of that, mister. We got him under control. Lee Chuck's a tough hombre, but there's no need to shoot him."

"Let him, Floyd. It'd save us the trouble of throwing Lee Chuck out."

Slocum's vision cleared. Two stewards clung tenaciously to Lee Chuck's arms, keeping the giant from finishing the deadly task he had begun. He aimed his six-shooter at the Chinaman's heart, then lowered the pistol, knowing the same stewards holding Lee Chuck would be the first to turn him over to the San Francisco police for murder, no matter what they said about gunning down their mountain of trouble.

He thrust the six-shooter back into his holster and tried to stare down the giant Celestial. Lee Chuck refused to blink. Trying to fathom the thoughts going on behind those dark orbs proved impossible. Lee Chuck knew his position was too secure. Slocum considered asking the stewards to let the Chinaman go so they could have it out once and for all, bare-knuckled and no weapons. Then Slocum realized his quarrel wasn't with Little Pete's bodyguard. It was with Little Pete.

"You want him thrown in the hoosegow, mister?"

"Get him out of my sight," Slocum said. "And his boss, too."

"Little Pete? We been watching him, but he hasn't kicked up any dust lately."

"He's paying trainers and jockeys to fix the races. I think he's drugging the horses so the favorites tire fast and other racehorses not worth sending to the butcher win.''

''That'd kill a horse, giving it joy juice to make it run faster,'' a steward said. ''But then, if the horses like Irish Cloverleaf winning today are any indication, dead ones from years past might be out there in the winner's circle soon enough.''

''Little Pete's been getting too much of a free ride, Floyd,'' said another. ''Let's kick him out permanently.''

''We'd need the owners' permission to do that,'' the other steward said. He jerked hard when Lee Chuck tried to break free from his grip. ''That might not be much of a problem after we tell 'em what's going on, though. Nobody likes getting cheated, and if Mr. Keller says so, who's gonna argue with *him*?'' He shoved Lee Chuck and sent the Chinaman staggering toward a distant exit. The tight suit threatened to split apart across Lee Chuck's shoulders as he tensed his muscles. Then he grunted and sneered at Slocum. With more dignity than Slocum would have thought possible, the mammoth bodyguard walked away, head held high and looking as if he owned the entire Bay District Race Track rather than having been banned from it.

''Damned highbinders ought to be outlawed,'' grumbled Floyd, brushing off his hands.

''Highbinders?'' asked Slocum. He watched as Lee Chuck vanished through the distant gate. ''What are those?''

''You gotta be new to San Francisco, mister,'' Floyd said. ''Highbinders are them Chinee killers. They use hatchets and kill people with strangling cords.''

''Silk garrotes they use on their victims,'' supplied the other man. He made a face and a jerking motion as if tightening a rope around his neck. ''Nasty customers. They work for the tongs.''

''I've heard of them. Criminal gangs.''

''Not like the Sydney Ducks, no sir,'' Floyd said.

"They were convicts from Down Under. These Chinee might be criminals, but not too many of them have been convicted of anything serious. Too sneaky, they are. Mark my words, the day'll come when somebody wises up and bans the whole lot of them. All Chinamen." Floyd spat.

"What about this Little Pete? He dresses well for a criminal."

"Criminal? Little Pete?" Floyd shrugged. "Might be, but all I know is, he owns about the biggest shoe manufacturing company on the coast. He sells his wares from San Diego all the way up to Seattle."

"Yep, he's a legit businessman, though not many know it. Folks don't want to buy Chinee shoes," said the other. "I've heard tell his real name is Fong Chong. Don't know why he goes with a name like Little Pete."

"Why does a businessman need a bodyguard like that Lee Chuck?" Slocum asked. "He's got the look of a cold-blooded killer to him." Slocum touched his neck and knew how close he had come to being strangled to death.

"Well, let's say Little Pete's business isn't all legal, if you know what I mean," said Floyd, giving Slocum a broad wink. "None of the really rich people around here got their dough being shy about snookering others, but Little Pete's another kettle of fish."

"What's he do? Tong work?" Slocum watched the two men closely. Floyd was getting increasingly uneasy at the discussion, but the other man's eyes widened, whether in amazement or fear, Slocum couldn't quite tell.

"Heard tell he heads up something called the Gi Sin Seer." Floyd swallowed hard.

"What's that?" asked Slocum, but he saw Floyd had reached the end of the conversation. But his friend hadn't.

"They are a blackmail society. They find out nasty things about people and threaten them unless they pay."

"People?" scoffed Floyd. "I wouldn't call it that. Little Pete keeps that business down in Chinatown. Do you think any of the gentlemen coming to the Bay District

Race Track would put up with such behavior? Only the Chinamen have anything to fear, and who knows what secrets they want kept.''

''I never knew,'' the other steward said. Slocum decided it wasn't fear but admiration for such audacity that caused his response. ''Still, why let him into the track?''

''I can answer that,'' Slocum said dryly. He pictured a huge roll of greenbacks and knew the reason. For all the cheating Little Pete might do, he brought huge amounts of money to the track.

''Really?'' Floyd's companion wasn't too quick on the uptake. Or maybe, unlike Floyd, he wasn't being paid off.

''Money,'' Slocum said. ''I reckon he greases palms all the way in, just as he does when he reaches the trainers and jockeys to fix the races. The man is richer than the three of us combined.'' For Slocum to include himself wasn't hard, and the two stewards looked hardly more prosperous than he was at the moment.

''You hit that one right on the head, yes, sir,'' said Floyd. ''I've seen Little Pete bet a thousand dollars on a single horse.''

''But if he's really fixing the races, nobody will cotton much to that.'' Floyd's companion still hadn't twigged to the fact that his friend might be one of those paid off to let the head of the Gi Sin Seer into the track for a day's race fixing.

Slocum watched the two stewards walk off, arguing about approaching the owners with the request to bar Little Pete from the racetrack. What they did affected him not at all. He saw the last race of the day had gone off. Whether Little Pete had won with another fixed race, Slocum neither knew nor much cared. He was out eight hundred dollars and wanted it back.

More than an hour passed before Slocum saw Little Pete exit from the racetrack, using a side exit. The Chinaman

entered a carriage driven by Lee Chuck and motioned for
his bodyguard to drive on. Slocum followed at a distance,
riding slowly as the two Celestials headed toward San
Francisco. He wasn't sure what he intended to do—other
than get his money back—but he wasn't going to bull his
way in without knowing what dangers he faced. Slocum
rubbed his bruised neck and knew he couldn't let Lee
Chuck get the upper hand again.

Little Pete seemed in no hurry to return to town, his
bodyguard driving him up and down streets. Slocum settled down and simply trailed the pair, knowing it wouldn't
do him any good to rush the matter. Too often he had
seen others come to bloody ends because they grew impatient.

As if coming to a decision, Little Pete suddenly headed
straight back for the middle of San Francisco. The clack-
ing of wheels over cobblestones turned to more sedate
whooshing as the carriage reached Dupont Gai, the street
running straight through the middle of Chinatown. Slocum couldn't help noticing the stir Little Pete's passage
caused. The well-dressed businessman might have been
visiting royalty for all the deference shown.

Men jumped from the path of the carriage and bowed
low, their queues flopping about as their heads bobbed up
and down. Some even dropped to their knees and banged
their heads against the ground. Kowtowing, Slocum had
heard it called. Such behavior was reserved for only those
with incredible position and power.

Slocum knew he had been right not confronting Little
Pete directly. The stewards had mentioned the criminal
tong. From the deference shown to the passing horse race
fixer, Little Pete's power extended to the deepest levels
of Chinatown. How Slocum was going to get his money
became more of a puzzle, but it was one he was willing
to solve.

The carriage made a sudden right turn onto Columbus.
Slocum urged his horse forward faster but found the going

difficult. Little Pete had passed down the middle of Dupont Gai with no trouble. Now the crush of an early-evening crowd forced Slocum to slow and often to simply stop. He stood in the stirrups and tried to keep the carriage in view but failed.

"Out of the way," Slocum shouted. He put his heels to the horse. It crow hopped and tried to balk, but Slocum kept urging it forward. The horse finally pushed apart the crowd and reached the corner of Dupont Gai and Columbus.

As Slocum had feared, Little Pete had vanished.

Riding down the broad street took him away from Chinatown at an angle. Soon he rode along the Embarcadero, surrounded by sailors fresh from their sailing ships and less savory sorts willing to prey on anyone showing the least weakness. Tall-masted ships creaked against the piers and in the distance, Slocum saw three ships raising huge canvas sails as they headed toward distant ports. But nowhere did Slocum see Little Pete or his behemoth bodyguard.

By the time he turned west along Market Street, Slocum knew he had lost the Chinaman and his servant. Cursing softly, he wondered if it would be worth the effort collecting what was owed him. The brief argument with himself was quickly resolved. He wasn't the kind to let anyone cheat him this way. He'd find Little Pete and get the money from him.

On impulse, Slocum began wending his way through the streets, heading for Portsmouth Square. The crowds thinned for a few blocks and then grew in size as he neared the square. On one corner stood a wild-eyed man waving a straight razor about and screaming about the hordes of Chinese streaming into the country. If Slocum had to choose, the wild-eyed man would have been on the next boat out, not any of the Celestials he ranted against.

"Except for Little Pete," Slocum allowed. Some men

didn't deserve any consideration, no matter their color. Slocum felt he had only scratched the surface of the rotten exterior of the Chinese highbinder's activities.

He let himself get caught up in the carnival atmosphere around Portsmouth Square: hawkers selling their bogus wares, street performers juggling and performing various feats of legerdemain, and dozens of storefront businesses operating as if it were noon rather than almost eight o'clock at night. San Francisco might catnap, but it never slept.

Slocum's attention turned to one window neatly painted with the name, Portsmouth Square Rescue Society. He realized he had unconsciously come in that direction because Beatrice Keller had mentioned working there. The interior of the storefront was dark. The people who toiled daily to take care of penniless Chinese sojourners had gone home for the night. Slocum let out a sigh. He had not expected Beatrice to be here so late at night, but some small hope had still burned within him.

She was one beautiful woman, and he wouldn't mind seeing her again.

"Here, come here to see the finest in Chinese opera, the best in puppet shows, jugglers, every form of entertainment from the distant Orient," came the cry from a man dressed in gaudy silks. "Come see the Hook Took Troupe, the finest performing group in all of China!"

Slocum rode closer and watched as jugglers performed incredible feats, colorful silk ribbons tied to weighted sticks that spun through the air in a dizzying cascade that only got more complex as several jugglers joined in. Four men juggled, then five, and eventually six, the twirling sticks having balls and even knives added to the stack of spinning, turning objects in the air.

Slocum was amazed at their skill, but his attention was pulled away by several young women standing near the edge of the makeshift stage. They spoke in hushed tones among themselves, mouths shielded by petite hands. Their obvious anxiety caused Slocum to look around. Through the fluttering curtains on the stage, he saw another Chinese girl, hardly eighteen, speaking to Beatrice Keller.

From the way they stood and the way Beatrice gestured, Slocum knew this was no casual conversation. The lovely blond gestured as if she wanted the Chinese girl to leave right away. The small shakes of the head and the expression on the girl's face told Slocum that Beatrice would never get the Celestial to budge.

He urged his horse around to the side of the stage and dismounted. He had no prospects and nothing else to do but hunt for Little Pete. Seeing Beatrice again had perked up his spirits a mite. If he could help her out, it might do him a world of good and change his attitude even more.

"Miss Keller," he called. He got no reply, so he climbed the three steps and went behind the curtains. Beatrice and the Chinese girl still spoke in guarded tones, but the other women had vanished. Slocum could see only a part of the stage and thought they might be performing. From the loud applause from the crowd, the Hook Took Troupe was popular.

"Beatrice!" he called, finally getting the blond's attention. A flash of fright crossed her lovely features, then faded when she recognized him. He strode over.

"Mr. Slocum, I hardly expected to see you tonight," she said. Beatrice glanced at the girl, who seemed to fold into herself as if this would make her entirely invisible. "This is Ah So."

"What?" Slocum wasn't sure he heard Beatrice properly.

"That's her name. I have been trying to convince her to come with me. She is in great danger if she remains."

"Why's that? The crowd seems peaceful enough, though there are enough sailors who might get rough if they knocked back a few drinks."

"Drunken sailors are not Ah So's problem," Beatrice said. She seemed tossed on the horns of a dilemma. "Mr.

Slocum, I have no reason to trust you. You are an acquaintance I met in passing, but I find myself in a position where I must appeal to you for help.''

''What can I do?''

''We need to reach—'' Beatrice never finished her sentence. The words ended in a gurgle as a hand clamped firmly over her mouth and dragged her back. Ah So let out a small cry and then she, too, was pulled toward the rear of the stage by a man dressed in a quilted cotton suit of the purest coal black.

Slocum never asked questions. He dived forward, tackling the Chinaman trying to abduct Beatrice. He found himself at the bottom of a pile of punching, kicking highbinders. One blow glanced off the side of his head, stunning him. Another smashed squarely into his temple. Everything went black around him.

3

His ears rang from loud cheers, but whatever poked John Slocum in the belly hurt worse. The deafening cries were annoying, but the object sticking him in the gut *hurt*. This forced him back from the brink of unconsciousness. He pushed himself off a pile of Indian clubs used by the Hook Took Troupe in their juggling and rubbed at the spot where the blunt end of one had tried to enter his stomach. He sat up and shook his head clear of the cobwebs.

It took him several seconds to remember what had happened and why he was in this sorry state. He shot to his feet, hand resting on the butt of his six-gun. The highbinders who had attacked him and kidnapped Beatrice and Ah So were nowhere to be seen.

Slocum went to the edge of the curtain and peered out. The Chinese performers worked their way through juggling objects to tossing each other around in a dazzling display of coordination, skill, and strength. But it took him only a few seconds to know Ah So was not among them. And in the crowd watching so approvingly, not a single face approached Beatrice Keller's in beauty. He turned and went to the rear of the makeshift stage. Jumping down, he ducked under the canvas and walked out into the middle of Portsmouth Square.

Dozens of people milled around behind the stage, but most were in front, watching the performance. Slocum approached a sailor who was trying valiantly to remain on his feet but was failing because too much rotgut had trickled down his gullet. The old sailor waved an empty bottle about as if the skies might open and it would rain down more whiskey for him.

"Did you see two women, a blond and a Chinese girl?" Slocum demanded. He grabbed the sailor by the shoulders and spun him around. The man's breath was enough to knock over a mule.

"See 'um? Danged near ran me over, they did. They was with some Chinee fellas."

"Where'd they go?"

The sailor gestured to the far side of the square. Slocum would have demanded more from the salt except that he saw two of the highbinders who had grabbed Beatrice and Ah So drifting down a side street. He sprinted for the far side of the square and dashed down the alleyway. He slowed and came to a stop when he didn't immediately see the hatchet men ahead of him. Stories of how they use hatchets on their victims—and garrotes—returned to instill a tad of caution in his headlong pursuit.

Slocum crouched down, listening hard. Tracking in the middle of San Francisco was no different from following quarry in the middle of the Montana forests or in the Sonora Desert. He had entered the enemy's territory, and he had to be more clever than they were.

Small rustling sounds told Slocum where wharf rats dined. He moved forward slowly, duck-walking to keep a low profile. He felt the presence of others. Hair rose on the back of his neck, but he kept moving. Whether a flash of light on the knife blade warned him or Slocum simply anticipated the attack through some sixth sense didn't matter. He drew his six-shooter and fired point-blank into the highbinder's belly when the man attacked.

The hatchet man collapsed in the center of the alley. The six-gun's report and the groan of their companion dying brought out three others. Slocum got off two quick shots, winging two of the attackers but not stopping them. One hit high and the other low, carrying Slocum backward. He kicked out and decked one. The other slid away like quicksilver. Slocum gave him no time to use the wicked knife flashing back and forth in his hand.

Another shot dispatched him. Slocum spun about and kicked, catching the fallen man in the head with the toe of his boot.

Then he found the third highbinder swarming over him like ants from an anthill finding a picnic. Hands grabbed wildly and feet kicked, but Slocum refused to give up. He danced back and let a knife cut the air in front of his face. Then Slocum got his six-shooter up and fired again, hitting the highbinder smack in the middle of the face.

A door opened down the alley and a head poked out. Slocum couldn't see the man's features, but a long queue told him this was another Chinaman. The Celestial made a quick survey of the scene and slammed the door behind him. Slocum heard a locking bar fall into place. No amount of battering would ever get that door open.

Crouching again to give as little a target as possible, Slocum reloaded, then tucked his pistol into his holster. He looked up and saw a window above him. Piling a few barrels on top of each other, he scrambled up. The window was locked, but Slocum rammed his elbow through the filthy glass and quickly released the lock. He tumbled into the room and came to his feet, hand on his six-gun again.

"No, please, you can't do this. My papa is an important man. He'll give you whatever you want, for me, for Ah So!"

Slocum recognized Beatrice's voice. From the curt grunt she garnered in response, he knew the Celestials were not moved. He had no idea what prompted the kidnapping, but taking Ah So along with Beatrice Keller told him more was involved than simple ransom. Beatrice was worth thousands of dollars. What would a young female performer in the Hook Took Troupe be worth to anyone?

The sound of a fist hitting a face sent Slocum to the door, where he opened it a crack and peered down the stairs. He saw two highbinders pacing about, arms crossed over their chests. A third one cocked his fist back and threatened Beatrice again.

"Don't strike me, you ruffian!" she cried.

Slocum fired when the highbinder started to hit her again. The Chinaman fell forward over her, producing a new shriek of outrage from the blond. But Slocum wasn't paying attention to Beatrice any longer. He positioned himself at the head of the stairs, trying to get a good shot at the other two hatchet men.

Ah So called out, warning Slocum. He bent double and rolled forward as a highbinder sneaked up on him from behind. The man tumbled over Slocum's shoulder and crashed down the stairs, acting like a bowling ball when he tumbled into the two men below, who were trying to mount the steps.

Slocum fired again, more to get their attention than to kill. Dark eyes peered at him, eyes without fear or any sign of emotion. Never had Slocum seen more emotionless, cold eyes staring at him.

"Back," he said, motioning with his six-shooter. The three highbinders scuttled like crabs to the far side of the dusty room. Slocum went to where Beatrice struggled under the dead weight of the Chinaman he had shot. Grabbing the queue, Slocum tugged hard and pulled the man off. He sank to the floor. Slocum had blasted his spine into shards with his single shot.

"John, thank heavens!" sputtered Beatrice. She started to gush out her thanks, but Slocum had to stop her. They were in serious straits, and he had no idea how to get them out of it without murdering three prisoners.

"Not now," he warned. Slocum picked up a fallen knife and slashed Beatrice's ropes. He handed her the knife and indicated she should free Ah So. Slocum tried to figure what to do with the three men who sat cross-legged in the corner, saying nothing and staring emotionlessly at him. His trigger finger tapped lightly. He had shot men in cold blood before, but it always tore at his gut. He had no compunction about shooting someone trying to kill him, or even killing for a good reason.

Fact was, Slocum had no idea what was going on and wasn't inclined to shoot these three men without knowing.

"Do something with them and let's go, John," urged Beatrice. She and Ah So worked to open the heavy wooden plank locking the door.

"What do you suggest? Kill them outright?"

"What? No!" Beatrice's hand flew to her mouth in horror. "I didn't mean that. Why, can you just shoot them in the legs so they won't follow? We must get away. We *must* or all is lost."

"How about tying them with the ropes over there?" Slocum pointed to a pile of rope.

"A splendid idea. But I'm not sure I know how to tie knots."

Before Slocum could say anything, Ah So pushed past. She whipped the ropes around and quickly secured the men. The three highbinders stared at her with something approaching awe. Slocum wondered if Chinese performers weren't supposed to know how to tie knots. He pushed it from his mind as he opened the door and peered into the alleyway.

"All clear," he said. "Where are we going? To your house?" he asked Beatrice.

"No!" The blond appeared more agitated now that they had escaped. "That is not a good idea, John. My father would never permit me to bring a . . . refugee home."

Slocum knew what Beatrice really meant. Henry Keller

had no time or tolerance for what he probably considered interlopers and sojourners coming to America to earn a few dollars before going home to China.

"Where do we go?" he asked. He had pushed the women down the alley in the direction away from the highbinders he had killed earlier. They came out onto Powell Street where Beatrice looked around in desperation.

"I don't know where we are."

Slocum told her, pointing east toward Portsmouth Square. "We can get back to your office. I saw it earlier tonight." Even as he spoke, he remembered his horse. By now it had been stolen, along with his belongings. Slocum counted this as an additional debt Little Pete owed him. If he hadn't hunted for the boss of the Gi Sin Seer, he wouldn't have gotten involved with Beatrice's and Ah So's problems.

The thought of the Chinese woman made him study her more closely. She stood silently, eyes downcast. Her hands were clasped in front of her, and she seemed to be nothing more than a servant waiting for her master to give a command.

"You want to get her back to the performing troupe?"

"No!" Beatrice's frightened outburst told him that more rested on Ah So than appeared. "It would be dangerous, too dangerous for her. I tried to convince her to flee back when we were grabbed by the tong killers."

"You know who they were?"

"Of course," Beatrice said in disgust. "I am no fool, no matter what you think of me."

"I think you're pretty gutsy," Slocum said truthfully.

"What else?" She turned her emerald eyes on him. He felt himself thinking with his balls rather than his brain. He pushed such notions away. She was high society, the best San Francisco had to offer. Slocum didn't even have two nickels to rub together.

"I think you're real pretty, too," he said. "And it's the

middle of the night, and we are in considerable danger unless you have somewhere specific to go.''

Beatrice smiled at him, then took a look around as if for the first time. The shadows moving across the street seemed to come closer. Everywhere around them lay unknown peril.

''There's a place we can go on Nob Hill. I don't know where that is, exactly, from here.''

Slocum turned and pointed toward the north. That was as close as he could get without knowing more of Beatrice's destination.

''Wait a minute,'' he said. Slocum went and hailed a passing carriage. He spoke briefly with the driver. The rig came over and the driver growled, ''Hurry up and get your asses in. I ain't got the night, you know.''

''What a disagreeable man,'' Beatrice muttered as she let Slocum help her up into the carriage. Ah So's eyes widened when Slocum turned to assist her. She reached out a slender hand and permitted him to usher her into the carriage. He noticed how tiny her feet were and how she stepped so carefully. Slocum silenced the driver's crude comments about both a blond and a Chinee whore with a cold glare.

The carriage bucked and started north along Powell, the horse straining to take the steep hill.

''I hope you've got a few dollars hidden away wherever we're going,'' Slocum said. He quickly explained how he had lost his horse and other belongings rescuing Beatrice and Ah So.

''I'm sorry. I shall see you are handsomely rewarded for your efforts,'' Beatrice said. Slocum wasn't sure exactly what form this reward would take, but anything would put him ahead of where he was now. He reached over and pulled down the canvas curtains, plunging the interior of the carriage into complete darkness. Ah So jumped.

''I have to,'' he explained. ''By now, those three have

gotten free and are hunting for us.'' The girl shivered once as if she had taken a serious case of the ague, then sat passively. The threat of pursuit frightened her, though she hid it well.

"Down that street,'' Beatrice said, heaving a sigh of relief. He enjoyed the sight of her breasts rising and falling under her crisply starched white blouse as she directed the driver up increasingly steep hills until they stopped in front of a dark, two-story house. "I'll get some money,'' she said, popping out.

Slocum had to caution the driver not to raise a ruckus. In a few minutes, a gas lamp filled the front room with pale illumination. Soon after, Beatrice returned with a wad of greenbacks rivaling the one Slocum had seen in William Considine's pocket at the racetrack.

"Here, sir, thank you for your service,'' Beatrice said, peeling off a few of the notes and handing them to the driver. The tone she used left no doubt the man had been summarily dismissed. Slocum had heard the tone before in those used to commanding servants.

"We will be safe here,'' Beatrice said, taking Ah So's hand and leading the girl up the path. Slocum followed a few paces behind, studying the grounds around the house. Weeds grew everywhere and the short picket fence circling the yard needed painting. The house itself was in better condition, but not by much. Everything gave the impression that the residents had seen better days, then moved on, taking nothing with them.

Inside, sheets covered the furniture and the single kerosene lamp cast a pale yellow glow in the front room.

"If you're worried about being seen, draw the curtains,'' Slocum suggested.

"Good, yes, we need to do that.'' Beatrice bustled about pulling closed the curtains. "I'll see Ah So settled.''

"While you're doing that, I'll scout outside to see if anyone followed us.'' Slocum went through the few rooms on the first floor, finding only undisturbed dust and no prints leading upward to the bedrooms. Satisfied that the place was safe, he passed through the kitchen and sat on the back porch, waiting for his eyes to adapt to the dark again.

He saw a black cat chasing its prey through the weeds, then saw dozens of other small creatures coming and going. Their routine was undisturbed, satisfying Slocum that no one lurked nearby. Getting to his feet, he made his way out the back into an alley. Fifteen minutes of prowling convinced him their carriage had not been followed by the highbinders, but he knew a few dollars or a single flash of a knife or hatchet would loosen the driver's tongue.

If the tong wanted Ah So, it would not be too hard figuring out where she had gone.

Slocum circled the block and made his weary way up the front steps again. The door had not been locked. He slipped inside, secured it behind him, and again patrolled the first floor. Ah So slept on a couch in what might have been a library or study. He pulled the door to the room shut and again looked at the stairs going to the second story.

A single set of footprints in the dust showed that Beatrice had gone upstairs. He followed slowly, checking every riser for creaking. Such could provide a few seconds' warning if the highbinders found the house and tried to take Beatrice again.

Slocum paused at one door, his hand on the cut-glass doorknob. From within came faint sounds he could not immediately identify.

"Beatrice?" he called softly. No answer. "Beatrice?" He spoke louder, wondering what was going on. "Beatrice!" he shouted when he heard a window being raised, woodenly protesting every inch of the way.

He gave the doorknob a savage twist and spun into the room. His eyes went wide, his heart hammered hard, and he stopped dead in his tracks at what he saw.

4

"Beatrice!"

"I thought you were never going to come in, John. Do you like what you see?"

Slocum was at a loss for words as he watched the slender blonde turn slowly. She was as naked as a jaybird. The creaking he had heard was the woman raising the dirt-caked window to let in a steady flow of moonlight that bathed her body, caressing every sleek curve and every wondrous bulge. When she stood still, the moonlight cast tiny shadows off her nipples, erect and begging for attention.

But Slocum found himself unable to figure out where to look. Her narrow waist flared out into very womanly hips. Nestled between her silky thighs was a patch of blonde fur that was turned into quicksilver by the light. The gentle breeze blowing into the musty room caused her long blonde hair to flow around her lissome body, masking some parts but still allowing him a full view of her nudity.

He felt himself responding.

"Come in and close the door. We don't want to disturb Ah So." She moved to him like a pale ghost floating through the night, but the womanly fingers pressing here and there were anything but ghostly. He grew even harder as her fingers stroked his crotch.

"Is this what you want to do?" he asked, the words husky.

"Yes, John, it is. I've wanted you from the moment I saw you at the track." Then all words were cut off as she threw her arms around his neck and pulled him close for a passionate kiss.

Slocum felt hard nipples pressing into his chest. The sexy woman moved even closer, her leg lifting and circling his waist to pull him to her graceful body and trap him erotically. Slocum's tongue dueled with hers as they mingled, darting from mouth to mouth. He ran his hands down her silky-skinned back and cupped her taut buttocks.

Lifting her by these sexy handles, he carried her to the bed. He gently placed Beatrice on the bed and worked to get his shirt off. She helped, and sent buttons flying across the floor. He fumbled a moment and got his gun belt off. Somehow, her nimble, dancing fingers got him out of his pants far faster then he ever could have.

For this, Slocum was glad. His erection jerked upright, straining and painful against the tough denim of his jeans. Beatrice caught her breath the instant she freed him from the cloth prison.

"So big, John. I had hoped."

Then she stopped talking and applied her lips to the tip of his manhood. Slocum gasped and turned weak in the knees as her tongue laved up and down the thick stalk. He ran his fingers through her lush blonde tresses and drew her face downward. She began bobbing her head and he guided her in the rhythm he found the most exciting. Only when her mouth had pushed him to the limits of his endurance did he pull away.

"No more," he gasped. In spite of the cool breeze blowing in from San Francisco Bay, he was drenched with sweat. Beatrice's green eyes twinkled wickedly in the moonlight.

"What's wrong, John? Afraid you can take it but not dish it out?"

"I'll show you how I can dish it out," he said, shoving her back onto the bed. Beatrice laughed in delight as he began working up the insides of her thighs, his tongue touching here and there, leaving wet patches. His lips brushed the blonde thatch and then slipped higher, across the gentle dome of her belly all the way to her breasts.

He caught first one and then the other nipple between his lips. Sucking hard, he gave her some of the pleasure she had already given him. But Slocum knew he could not continue much longer. He was on fire inside. The pressures mounting in his loins demanded release.

"More, John. I want more from you," sobbed out a desire-racked Beatrice. "You can give it to me. I know you can!"

She reached down and grabbed his thick stalk, pulling him inexorably toward the furry triangle he had passed over with his mouth. He let her draw him upward. The tip of his shaft brushed strands of dewy-moist fleece, then he plunged balls deep into her tight interior.

His hips went wild when he buried himself all the way. He could not hold back an instant longer. This suited Beatrice just fine. She lifted her buttocks off the bed and ground her crotch into his as he slid back and forth with increasing haste and need. Every inch of his length tingled and felt as if it had been dipped in liquid fire. All around, her tight muscles clamped on him, milked him, squeezed him, until the hot tide in his balls could not be denied.

Seconds before he spilled his seed, Slocum felt the lovely blonde arch her back under him and cry out in release. He was lost in a sexual world a thousand miles away. He continued pumping until he turned flaccid. Then he collapsed forward onto the woman's chest, her breasts cradling his face.

"You were superb, John. I knew you would be. Everything about you shows your . . . competence."

"I was inspired," he said.

Beatrice laughed. He moved so that he could take her in his arms. Side by side they lay bathed in the silvery moonlight, letting the increasingly chill breeze from the bay blow over their sex-sweated bodies.

"I worried nothing would work out for me," Beatrice said. "For me and Ah So. Now I know it will."

Before Slocum could ask what it was she sought from the Celestial, he felt her fingers tangling in his chest hair, then moving lower. He didn't think he could respond again so soon, but Beatrice proved he was capable of more than he thought.

Noise of carriages outside woke Slocum just after sunup. Beatrice lay in the bed, a sheet half pulled over her. He saw how the sunlight turned her exotic moonlight beauty into something even richer. If possible, she was more beautiful in the full light of day. He pulled a sheet up over one exposed breast. She murmured in her sleep and turned, revealing the her long legs and the shapely swell of her buttocks. Slocum held back his impulse. They had enjoyed one another several times during the night. It was time for him to tend to other matters.

Little Pete owed him money, and he intended to collect it.

Dressing quickly, Slocum slipped out the door and went down the stairs, avoiding the creaking steps he remembered from the night before. Looking in on Ah So, he saw that the Chinese girl still slept. Slocum settled his gun belt around his hips and left through the rear door, not wanting to provoke comment being seen going out the front door.

He sucked in a deep breath of the brisk salt air, turned slowly, and got his bearings. The house was halfway up the slope of Nob Hill, a fancy section of town. The nearby houses were posh, not like the run-down one Beatrice had found. He would have to ask how this house had come to be so shabby in the midst of such obvious wealth. It certainly wasn't because Henry Keller lacked money. He could afford to lose ten thousand dollars at the racetrack and only be put out at the inconvenience. For Slocum, losing five hundred spelled the difference between eating and starving.

Long strides took him downhill in the direction of Chinatown. Finding Little Pete might be difficult, considering the fear the Chinese thug generated with his killing and blackmailing, but to Slocum's surprise, he had little trouble finding the Gi Sin Seer leader.

Little Pete's bodyguard was impossible to miss as he strutted along the street. The Celestials made way for the huge Lee Chuck, backing away and bowing and scraping. Slocum pressed himself into a narrow doorway and let Lee Chuck swagger by, then moved to follow him down Dupont Gai. Lee Chuck had no trouble with the crowd, but Slocum did. The Chinese bumped into him and kept him from closing the gap, but it also provided a bit of concealment, though Slocum stood head and shoulders above the shorter Celestials.

Lee Chuck went into store after store, meaty hand thrust out. Frightened store owners handed over sheaves of money, which Lee Chuck tucked into his pocket. Then he left the stores without a word. Slocum knew what would happen to any merchant refusing to pay the protection money. If Lee Chuck didn't beat the hell out of the man right away, a fire might start later that night or one of the merchant's family might have an unfortunate accident.

Slocum itched to put a bullet in Lee Chuck's head, but he held back. Removing the burly bodyguard would do nothing to stop Little Pete. Little Pete was the spider in the middle of the web controlling myriad illicit activities in Chinatown. When Slocum stepped on Little Pete, Lee Chuck would be nothing more than an annoyance.

For a moment, the crowd along the street parted, and Slocum saw his quarry. Little Pete stood on a street corner, arms folded and a smug expression on his face. He didn't see Slocum. He had eyes only for his bodyguard and the thick wad of greenbacks Lee Chuck carried.

Little Pete motioned for Lee Chuck to enter an alleyway. The two Chinese bandits vanished as Slocum dashed over. That much money had to cover his loss at the racetrack. He had no reason to take more than he had been cheated out of, even if the temptation to punish Little Pete by taking it all was great.

Maybe he would take his eight hundred dollars, then try to recover Henry Keller's ten thousand and give it to Beatrice. The notion pleased Slocum. It carried a certain straightforward justice to it.

He started to draw his Colt Navy when he saw that Little Pete and Lee Chuck were already backed against a brick wall, their hands high above their heads. Arrayed in a semicircle around them were four other highbinders, obviously unfriendly to Little Pete by the way they brandished their knives and six-shooters.

Singsong demands came from the would-be thieves, but neither Little Pete nor Lee Chuck appeared inclined to pass over their protection money.

"You Bo Sin Seer fools will never take over my territory," Little Pete said in his sibilant, menacing voice.

"He's right," Slocum said, cocking his six-shooter and pointing it at the leader of the highbinders facing Little Pete. "I want the money."

The momentary break of attention sent Lee Chuck into action. The huge Celestial reached out and grabbed the nearest highbinder and slammed him hard against the wall. The man's head was crushed like an eggshell. He slid down the brick wall, leaving behind a blood trail.

But Lee Chuck wasn't watching. He grabbed another knife-wielding hand and jerked hard, swinging the man around.

As the fight unfurled, the highbinder holding the pistol on Little Pete turned and got off a shot at Slocum. Slocum's return shot missed by inches, sending the gunman scurrying for shelter. Slocum got off two more shots before he realized the alleyway behind him had filled with blue-suited policemen.

One grabbed Slocum's gun from his hand and pushed him to one side.

"None of that now, boy-o," came the order. "We don't take kindly to people shootin' up our people, even if they are damned Chinee."

Slocum started to warn the policeman of the danger, but couldn't get the words out before Lee Chuck scooped up a fallen six-shooter and fired.

The bullet caught the policeman talking to Slocum in the back of the head. The man was dead by the time he hit the dirty alleyway.

If Slocum thought the bustle of lawmen was intense before, it was nothing compared to the rush of police now and the shrill whistling to summon still more armed specials patrolling Dupont Gai in groups of threes and fours.

Both Lee Chuck and Little Pete tried to run but found themselves bottled up in the alleyway. Little Pete surrendered first, but Lee Chuck realized his plight. He had shot a policeman from the back. He tried to fight his way free, but a dozen nightsticks flashed in the light and landed on any exposed portion of the Chinaman's body until he sank to the ground. Even then, the policemen did not stop beating and kicking the fallen man.

"Enough of that, lads," came a gruff voice. A man sporting captain's bars on his hard hat and collar tabs strode into the alley. He pushed the circle of police back and looked at Lee Chuck's battered body. The captain appeared to consider what to do. Then he whipped out a knife, reached down, and grabbed Lee Chuck's long queue.

Little Pete started to protest, but a nightstick in his belly silenced him. The captain made a single quick swipe with the knife and cut off the queue.

Slocum knew how the Celestials cherished their long pigtail. The police captain might as well have cut off Lee Chuck's balls.

Then Slocum realized that might follow. They were taking Little Pete's bodyguard to jail, along with his boss—and John Slocum.

"Come along now," one officer said, shoving Slocum out into the middle of Dupont Gai. The Chinese crowd faded away like mist in the morning sun.

"I didn't have anything to do with that," Slocum said. "I heard Little Pete say they were Bo Sin Seer."

"A tong fight, is it now?" the cop said, shoving Slocum down the street in the middle of a wedge of auxiliary special police. "Not too surprisin'. They are all the time killin' each other."

"He owes me money, and I only wanted to collect."

"What's a white man doin' bein' owed money by *his* like?" The policeman eyed Slocum critically. "There's more to this than you are sayin'. No matter, you saw poor ol' Danny O'Connor cut down back there. He's got a wife to mourn him." The cop shook his head. "Poor Katherine."

Slocum turned and saw other police stringing rope across the mouth of the alleyway. Already they had placed a pair of orange-painted barrels around the body as others walked the length of the alley, hunting for who knows what. Slocum had seen the killing and knew it was open-and-shut.

"Lee Chuck did the shooting," Slocum said. "There's no reason to take me to jail."

"Isn't there, now? We cannot have you ridin' off, never to be seen again. You're a witness, and perhaps more. You know more of them infernal Chinee's dealin's than you're lettin' on."

The police station at the edge of Chinatown had seen

better days, but Slocum doubted if there could ever be more prisoners locked up in the ramshackle cells. In some cells as many as ten Chinese were crowded shoulder to shoulder.

"In there, bucko," said the cop, shoving Slocum toward the rear. He went into the cell next to one already holding Little Pete and Lee Chuck. The crime lord's bodyguard lay on the floor, curled up and moaning. The police had done quite a job beating his head in.

"I want my money," Slocum called to Little Pete. The highbinder stared at Slocum, as if not seeing or hearing him, but a sly smile crept across his lips. Saying nothing, Little Pete turned and hunkered down at the far side of the cell. The others in his lockup shied from him, recognizing his power.

"What's your dealings with the like of Little Pete?" asked a man in Slocum's cell.

"He cheated me. I want my money."

"He *cheated* you?" The grizzled man laughed long and hard. "That's not all he's likely to do if you irritate him overmuch. He's a killer, pure and simple."

"And a blackmailer," chimed in another. "I heard tell he extorts money from all them Chinee up and down Dupont Gai."

"That's not his only source of money," said the first prisoner. "He owns a shoe company. Has white salesmen peddling his wares everywhere. See these?" The man turned and showed Slocum his high-topped leather shoes. "These are a pair of *his* shoes. Try and buy a pair he doesn't make anywhere up and down the Pacific Coast. Can't be done."

"Then why'd he feel he ought to do me out of eight hundred dollars?" asked Slocum.

A harsh laugh was all the answer he got from several prisoners in the jail. The talkative one said, "There's never enough money for *his* kind. He's no different from Huntington or Crocker, 'cept he's Chinee."

Slocum sagged to the cold stone floor, lost in his glum thoughts. Less than twenty minutes later, two jailers came back, swinging a key ring and rattling the bars with nightsticks.

"You're sprung, Pete. Get your skinny ass out of here." The jailer stepped back and let the leader of the Gi Sin Seer tong slip from the cell. Little Pete never glanced at his fallen bodyguard, who still moaned on the floor. He left the cellblock, head high and looking neither left nor right as he vanished.

"Hey, wait," Slocum called. "Why are you letting him go?"

"Bail, bucko, he's been bailed out," said one jailer.

"Who put up the money?" Slocum tried to figure out how Little Pete had gotten free so fast. Word had to spread up and down the length of Chinatown, but it hadn't been even a half hour.

The jail guard shrugged his massive shoulders. "Can't say who it was. Big fella, broad shoulders and expensive suit that threatened to pop at the seams."

"Was he taller than I am?" asked Slocum, standing to show off his six-foot height.

"That he was, bucko." With that, the guard left the cellblock.

Slocum sat back down, wondering why William Considine would bail out the highbinder.

5

Slocum slumped forward, dozing. Men came and went in his cell, but the door never opened for him. He wasn't sure what time of day it was, morning or night, after a spell. When the jailer came back, dragging his nightstick along the bars, it woke Slocum.

"You're outta here, bucko," the guard said, pointing at him.

"What? You decided to let me go?"

"Bailed out," the guard said.

"How?"

"No time for this jawin' now, lad. Out you go." The jailer shoved Slocum along the narrow walkway between the rows of iron-barred cells and into the police station lobby. To Slocum's surprise, he saw Beatrice Keller sitting on a hard bench, her hands folded primly in her lap. She looked up, and a slow smile crossed her lips.

"Mr. Slocum, I am glad to see you are unharmed."

"Now, now, Miss Keller, there's no call for sayin' things like that. You give our best regards to your pa," the jailer said. He tapped the bill of his cap with the side of his nightstick.

"You bailed me out? How'd you know I was in jail?"

Slocum blinked when he saw the sunlight outside. It was probably late afternoon. He thought he had been locked up for days, although it had been only hours.

"Word travels slowly at times," she said as she led the way from the police station, "and at others it has wings. I heard quickly."

"Did William Considine tell you?"

"What?" Surprise crossed her lovely face. "Why, no. Why do you say that, John?"

"Nothing," he replied. He took the small parcel she handed him. In it were his six-shooter and cross-draw holster. They felt good strapped around his middle again. "Are they pressing charges against me?"

"No, none. They had thought to hold you as a witness in a killing, but the captain allowed as to how they really had enough evidence against the killer. Lee Chuck, they called him. How did you get mixed up in this, John?" She seemed genuinely interested.

"Trying to collect a debt, that's all," he said. "You seem nervous."

"I am," Beatrice said, looking around while trying not to seem too obvious about it. "We are so close to Chinatown. The tongs are closing in on us. I can feel it."

"Us?" asked Slocum.

"Ah So and me."

"What's their interest in Ah So? I can understand why they might be involved in trying to kidnap you."

"Why's that?" she said, the impish grin returning to her lips for a moment.

"Quit fishing for compliments. Who wouldn't want to steal away such a beautiful woman? These are kidnappers, and your father's a rich man."

"They obviously do not understand him as well as I do. He would never pay ransom for me."

"Why not?"

She laughed, and it sounded harsh and ugly. "Papa does not believe in giving in to threats. They would only make further demands, he says. There would be no end to what they would do.''

"But, surely, to get his own daughter back . . ." Slocum let the sentence trail off. Whether Henry Keller would ransom Beatrice, he did not know, but Beatrice obviously thought her father would let her rot if anyone kidnapped her.

"I want your help hiding Ah So. We can do it in a few hours, after sundown. I can get a closed carriage. You drive us to somewhere we'll be safe. Across the bay to Oakland, perhaps.''

"A long drive," Slocum said. "We might get a ferry across.''

"Perhaps we can go north to Tiburon," Beatrice rambled on, not listening to him. She was so lost in her thoughts she almost walked past the house where Ah So hid. Slocum saw the Chinese girl peeking out from behind the thin curtains and wondered why the tong hadn't found her by now. She and Beatrice were terrible at hiding out.

"Down the street," he said, taking the woman by the arm. He steered the blond straight up the walk to the front porch and pushed her down into shadows formed by the slanting rays of the setting sun.

"John, what's wrong?" The blond's hand flew to her throat in a gesture of apprehension.

"Chinese down the street. Two of them. I don't think they saw you, but I'm sure they would flock here if they did. Get inside. Don't light any lamps, and tell Ah So to stay away from the windows. I saw her peeking out as we came up to the house.''

"Yes, right away." Beatrice knocked twice. Ah So peered out and immediately opened the locked door. "John—"

"I'll be back. Might take a while, but I'll be back. Lie low until you hear from me. And don't open the door for anyone else.''

"All right. Thank you.''

Slocum heard her parting words from the street. He turned sharply and cut across a neighboring yard to reach a side street. There he saw a half dozen more highbinders, but they milled around, not knowing where to go. This gave Slocum a little hope that Beatrice and Ah So might be safe. The Celestials hadn't located their quarry yet, but they knew the area to search.

That wasn't good, and Slocum wasn't sure if the advice he had given was so good, either. A few lights might keep the highbinders away. A dark house could appear to be a clever hiding place and draw them in to investigate. Slocum shrugged it off. Either way posed dangers for the women. The best thing he could do with so many of the tong hatchet men around was to find out what the hell was going on. That way, he could better aid Beatrice and get Ah So to safety. Right now, he simply did not know if anywhere was safe for the girl.

Slocum spent the better part of an hour walking up and down alleys in the Nob Hill area and counted no fewer than twelve hatchet men prowling about. He considered removing them one by one, but they were cautious and he knew he could never finish the task without sounding a hue and cry that would bring dozens more down on him. Better to let them hunt futilely for Beatrice and Ah So. If they failed to find their prey, they might quit and go home. Slocum didn't believe that for a minute, but it made for a comforting thought.

If he wanted to stop the manhunt, he had to get to Little Pete and put a stop to him.

Knowing it would be hard finding the head of the Gi Sin Seer after his bodyguard was locked up and a rival tong had tried to rob or kill him, Slocum walked back to Chinatown. By the time he got there, smoky lanterns along Dupont Gai filled the night with a curious mixture of sparks, light, and dense black clouds that turned the bustle of commerce into something exotic and incredibly dangerous.

Slocum tried standing on a street corner and watching for Little Pete, but this quickly proved impossible. All traffic around him came to a standstill. The Chinese simply stared at him, marking him as an outsider. Little Pete would have had to be blind not to notice Slocum's intrusion.

Walking slowly proved little better. The Celestials parted in front of Slocum, as if he had an invisible wall around him that knocked them out of the way. Slocum rounded a corner and found himself heading back toward Portsmouth Square and the bustle there. He remembered the Hook Took Troupe and considered questioning them about Ah So and why the tong would be after her. Perhaps he could find someone in the office of Beatrice's Rescue Society who might answer a few questions.

Before he got halfway there, a squad of police circled him and stopped him. Slocum considered how well they trapped him. The swinging nightsticks and the slungshots they bounced lightly against their palms told him he had no chance for escape. If he tried shooting his way out, they would kill him.

If they simply interrogated him, they might also kill him.

"Where ye be goin' this time of night?" asked a burly, red-faced cop with sergeant's stripes on his arm. A few others wore uniforms but most were specials, privately hired police who made more off extortion than they did salary.

"Down to Portsmouth Square," Slocum said. "I'm looking for a friend."

"Now who might it be that would meet with the likes of you?"

Slocum decided a bluff was the only way to get free. He boldly stared at the sergeant, then looked around at the others.

"It's not really a friend. Not exactly. I'm looking for my boss, Henry Keller."

The sergeant's eyes widened. "Now, is that a fact." He cleared his throat and moved a little closer. The smell of Irish whiskey on his breath about bowled over Slocum. "You tell him Sergeant Martin's on the watch for him, eh?"

"I'll do that."

"And mention that me lads here are all askin' what's become of their weekly salary."

Slocum kept from showing his astonishment at the idea that Henry Keller kept so many police on his payroll. He could fight a small army with these men. Somehow, Slocum doubted these were the only ones Keller paid off.

"I will. By the way, Sergeant, have you seen Considine tonight?" Slocum remembered how chummy Considine had been with Little Pete. He had, after all, bailed the tong boss out of jail. If Slocum couldn't find Little Pete directly, he might follow a trail left by Keller's right-hand man to the Gi Sin Seer leader.

"Mr. Considine, is it now?" Sergeant Martin scratched his balding head and pushed back his police cap with the tip of his nightstick. He glanced around the circle. No one spoke. "Reckon not this night. You might try over around Telegraph Hill."

"The fire tower yonder?" Slocum pointed toward North Beach, toward the Barbary Coast where few ever walked alone without being robbed, beaten, or killed.

"That's the one. Lily Hitchcock Coit's got quite a mansion up there. Rides with the firemen on every call, she does."

"But Considine would be out in a saloon?"

"He'd be in his usual haunts. The shootin' galleries, methinks. He frequents all of 'em in Chinatown, but the ones up near the Cobweb Palace out on Meiggs's Pier are more to his likin'. He's got quite an eye, that one." The sergeant hesitated as he gave Slocum an appraising once-over, gaze resting for a brief moment on the worn ebony butt of the Colt Navy slung so carefully at Slocum's left hip. ''Reckon the pair of you have that in common.''

''Could be,'' Slocum allowed. He nodded to the band of police as they walked away, ready to find someone else to accost. Slocum stood and watched them go, wondering why Henry Keller needed so many of the San Francisco constabulary on his payroll. He shrugged it off. Rich men got to be suspicious of everyone around them. This might be Keller's way of protecting himself.

Still, it didn't set right with Beatrice's assertion that her father would let her die rather than ransom her. What was paying off a police force but a kind of ransom? Or did Beatrice believe her father wouldn't pay but would send legions of the burly cops to find her and exact justice from her kidnappers?

Slocum turned northward and made his way into the Barbary Coast of San Francisco. In its day, this had been the most dangerous section of town anywhere in America. One gang after another claimed sovereignty over it, from the Hounds to the Sydney Ducks and then to the growing power of the Chinese tongs.

Now it was merely the most dangerous section of San Francisco. Ships pulled into the Embarcadero lacking crews. They often sailed with a full complement, their captains finding unwilling seamen drunk in deadfalls and bagnios.

Slocum left Chinatown, passing Pine Street, and he slowed when he heard gunshots. He remembered what the police officer had said about Considine enjoying firing a few rounds in the shooting galleries along Dupont Gai. Here were many more of the galleries, men lined up waiting their turn to take potshots at small targets. Slocum had little time for such posturing. When he got something in his sights, it wouldn't be a clay pipe or a wooden duck.

Slowing, Slocum glanced into one crowded gallery. A drunk was taking wild shots at the targets set up on a plank at the back of the long, narrow room. Slug after slug missed and tore into the iron sheet hung at an angle to deflect the bullets into the soft dirt on the floor.

"Keep firin'," urged the proprietor. "You're gettin' close enough now to scare 'em to death!" A roar of laughter went up in the crowd, but Slocum didn't join in. He saw a head above the shorter men gathered inside: William Considine.

Considine and another man were arguing. Finally, the other man reached into his pocket and drew out an envelope, which he handed to Considine. The tall, bulky man stuffed it into his coat pocket as he had done the wads of greenbacks he'd won at the Bay District Race Track.

Before Slocum could cross the room and accost Considine, another man hurried over. This small, mousy man's furtive gestures told Slocum of great fear, yet he stood in front of Considine and whispered rapidly. Considine nodded once and handed a few greenbacks to the man. The timid man counted the bills, bobbed his head up and down like a hen pecking corn, and hastily left.

Slocum had no idea what business Considine conducted, but it required a steady stream of men, most giving him money and a few selling information. Slowly crossing the room and edging closer, Slocum overheard one man's report.

"I know it's wild soundin', Mr. Considine, but it's true. Miz Grant's a tippler."

"The head of the temperance union?" Considine's eyebrows went up.

"God's truth, sir. I seen it with my own eyes. If this ever got out, she'd be ruined."

"Think of what that would do to her husband," mused Considine. "He'd likely pay a pretty penny to keep his reputation—and hers—from getting besmirched by scandal." Considine gave the man a crisp ten dollar bill.

Even as the greenback changed hands, Considine looked up. His dark eyes fixed on Slocum's cold green ones. As if the man were an open book, Slocum read the emotions racing across Considine's face: surprise, fear, anger, and downright hatred.

Slocum went for his six-shooter even as Considine was sticking his hand under his left arm to pull the six-gun he holstered there. What the man's game was, Slocum didn't know, but he suspected it was illegal and at odds with anything Henry Keller might approve of.

Considine's round tore past Slocum's ear and flew toward the rear of the shooting gallery. The round must have knocked over a target. A cheer went up, and Slocum heard the proprietor say, "That's the first target you hit tonight. I'm gonna give you a drink on the house!"

The poor marksman put down his six-shooter and accepted the drink, but Slocum hardly noticed. He ducked as Considine got off another round intended to bury itself between his eyes. Slocum returned fire, his slug going wild. Then it was too late. William Considine slipped out a side door into the chilly San Francisco night.

Slocum shoved through patrons of the shooting gallery and ran after the fleeing Considine. He ducked low and swung around, six-gun ready for action if Considine laid a trap for him.

He had come into an alleyway that stretched to a far street lighted by gas lamps. Between the door and the street was only a long stretch of emptiness. Slocum whipped around, Colt ready to fire. The darker section of the alley was equally empty.

He had lost Considine and his conduit to Little Pete.

6

Slocum slammed his six-shooter back into his holster and stalked to the end of the alley. He looked up and down Lombard Street, hunting for any trace of Considine. In the throng of drunken sailors, whores propositioning any man walking by, vendors hawking their wares, and a general crush of people, there was no way he could find William Considine or Little Pete.

After checking a half dozen other shooting galleries, Slocum gave up. A few people had seen Considine recently, but no one fessed up to seeing him that night. Every inquiry about Little Pete brought only stony silence, if not outright fear.

Long hours passed. It was almost midday by the time Slocum gave up and knew he had to follow a different trail if he wanted Considine in his sights again. Trudging the miles back up to Nob Hill where Beatrice and Ah So hid, Slocum followed the back ways and occasionally doubled around to see if anyone tracked him. The closer he got to the house, the more cautious he became, remembering the hordes of highbinders hunting Ah So.

This triggered questions anew in Slocum's head. Why was Beatrice helping Ah So run, and what was the young girl running from? The tongs? Did Little Pete and his Gi Sin Seer want her? The Bo Sin Seer? Most vexing of all, no matter what Beatrice thought of her father, he was the obvious source of both money and aid in getting the girl out of San Francisco and away from whatever threatened her.

A new question blossomed when he thought of William Considine. Was this the reason Beatrice was leery of going to her father? Did she fear Considine and his business connection with Little Pete?

All Slocum really decided was that he didn't know enough to even ask the right questions. He would find out more from Beatrice before pushing any farther. His sole intent was collecting money from Little Pete that had been stolen at the racetrack by the Celestial's horse drugging and jockey payoffs.

The neighborhood seemed quiet, even sleepy, though it was just a few minutes after noon. Slocum slipped into the backyard and shoved his way through the weeds, noting that none had been bent down. If anyone had approached the house since he left, it was by some other route.

He tapped lightly on the rear door and called, "Beatrice, it's me, Slocum. Let me in."

The curtain pulled back a few inches to reveal Ah So's wide, ebony dark eye. She hastily opened the door and stepped back, bowing deeply. For some reason, this irritated the hell out of Slocum.

"Don't go bowing and scraping around me like that," he said irritably. "Where's Miss Keller?"

Ah So looked up hesitantly, then dropped her eyes again. Her head shook slightly, the only answer Slocum was likely to get.

"Do you speak English? Understand it?"

He knew she understood what he said. He read it in the set to her body, even if she kept her face completely impassive. Ah So would have made a great poker player. Right now, all he wanted were answers.

When it became obvious he wasn't going to get any reply, Slocum went into the front room and looked around. It took only a few seconds for him to figure out Beatrice had left.

"Do you expect her back soon?" Slocum asked.

Ah So pointed to the bare kitchen table. Slocum understood. Beatrice had left to fetch some food. He didn't blame her, but he wished she had waited for him to escort her. The sound of footsteps on the front walk took him to the window, and he saw Beatrice hurrying up. She carried a single bag. Beatrice was startled when he opened the door for her.

"Oh, John, it's you. I didn't know when you would return."

"Get inside," he said, taking her arm and almost dragging her out of sight. "I don't know what happened to the highbinders I spotted last night, but since they haven't found you, it's a sure bet they haven't given up."

"I was careful," she said. Beatrice handed Ah So the bag of food. The Chinese girl took it and glided away toward the kitchen on her tiny, slippered feet.

"I need some answers," he said, but from the far-off look in her eyes, he knew he wasn't likely to get any.

"My father's being strange again," she said, working to take off her hat. She dropped her white gloves on a table beside the door. "This happens now and then, but when I spoke with him this morning, he was downright erratic."

"Erratic?"

"Why, yes, John. He could not concentrate. And he gave me money when I asked for it. He never does that unless he is mightily distracted. Something is worrying him, but he would not discuss it."

"Then let's discuss you and William Considine."

"What do you mean?" This got Beatrice's full attention. She turned around, and her green eyes flashed angrily. Slocum wanted to know why.

"When are the two of you getting married?"

"Married?" She sputtered indignantly, laughed, then sobered, and a storm cloud of anger formed. "Is he telling people that again? How dare he!"

"You're not engaged?"

"Hardly. I want nothing to do with him. He is an odious man. I do *not* understand why Papa continues to employ him." Beatrice crossed her arms over her chest. This pushed up her ample breasts and sent a momentary pang of memory of the night they had spent together through Slocum's brain and body.

"What's his link with Little Pete?"

"Considine? Why, I don't know. I wasn't aware he even knew Little Pete." The notion caused Beatrice to blanch. Slocum knew there was more she wasn't telling, and he was getting tired of trying to pry every little detail from her.

"Why is Ah So running? Who's after her?"

"You sound like a policeman. Where is your nightstick to beat the truth out of me?" She stamped her foot, anger causing her to flush now, replacing the pallor caused by the notion that Considine and Little Pete were in cahoots.

Before Slocum could respond, Ah So came into the room. She bowed and held out a plate of food. Slocum couldn't even identify most of the items there, but it was obvious she handed it to him. For the first time, Slocum took notice of how his belly grumbled. He couldn't remember the last food he had eaten. He accepted the plate from the Chinese girl and stared at it.

"Do you want chopsticks?" asked Beatrice, her good humor returning.

"I've seen Chinamen use them, but a plain old knife and fork's good enough for me," he said. Ah So quickly left and returned with the eating utensils. Slocum settled at the table in the dining room and ate hungrily. He hadn't a clue what he stuffed into his mouth, but he chewed with some satisfaction.

"That's good," he told Ah So, figuring she would understand but would not reply. A small smile danced at the corners of her mouth as she bowed and backed from the room.

"She's too damned subservient," Slocum said, watching her leave. Try as he might, he could not figure out why there was such a fuss over her. Ah So was no different from a hundred other Chinese girls he had seen.

"That's her way," Beatrice said, "but I agree that she ought to learn more modern ways of behavior."

Slocum snorted. "Don't go too far. Next thing you know, she'll want to vote."

"What's wrong with that?" From the flush rising to Beatrice's cheeks, Slocum knew he had stepped into a pit of rattlers all hissing and snapping at him. "Wyoming is considering allowing women to vote. Suffrage is an important issue."

"Among others," Slocum said, laying out the bait.

"What others?" Beatrice was primed and ready for a fight.

"For instance, what's so special about Ah So?"

Beatrice clamped her mouth shut, realizing he had lured her into almost revealing too much of her dealings with the Chinese girl.

"This is complicated, John. You know the tongs want her. I tried to understand, but my grasp of her language is minimal. I do know she is in trouble, and I have devoted my life to helping people like her."

"The Rescue Society?"

"Yes. John, will you help get her out of San Francisco tonight? To a place in Oakland?"

"We'd have to use the ferry or go down the bay and back up the other side. That would take more than a day. Longer," he said. Slocum tried to figure out his chances of finding Little Pete and getting his money if he took time from the hunt to escort Beatrice and this silent, subservient girl across the bay to Oakland.

"We dare not take the ferry. The tong has eyes everywhere along the docks. They immediately seize new arrivals and force them into membership."

"You mean they extort what money they have from the emigrants," Slocum said sourly. He had seen this done too many times in too many places. Somehow, though, he couldn't feel too bad about the Chinese. They weren't here to settle. They came only to work a few years, then return to China.

He had even heard of some who scrimped and saved what they called bone money. If they died before they were able to return to China, their bones were shipped back for burial. This didn't set well with Slocum. If they came to a new country, they ought to make it their own, even to having their bodies buried here.

"Sojourners," he muttered.

"What's that, John?" Beatrice looked up from her plate, almost as spotless as his.

"Nothing. If you can get the carriage, we can leave after sundown."

"I am not sure exactly where to get one," Beatrice said.

"I don't have any money. Little Pete did me out of it at the racetrack." Admitting this galled Slocum. It only caused the burr under his saddle to irritate him a bit more.

"Oh, John, how thoughtless of me. When I said I'd see that you were paid for your services, I hope you didn't think I meant to cheat you."

"The other night was plenty good pay. More than I expected," he said.

"But not all you want, I trust," she countered. Beatrice smiled her wicked smile, then reached into her purse and drew out a thick sheaf of greenbacks. After giving her plate to Ah So, she handed the scrip to Slocum. "That ought to cover our expenses."

He riffled through the bills. Almost a hundred dollars. A young fortune but still nowhere near what Little Pete owed him.

"I'll see to the carriage rental and get some food, too, for the trip. Be ready out back just after sundown."

"Is that wise? Perhaps we ought to wait until it is much darker," Beatrice suggested.

"If the highbinders mosey around in the light, your neighbors will shoo them away. After it gets darker, well, that's *their* time," he said, meaning the highbinders. "No one will venture out and question them and live to tell about it."

"I see. We start when there is some protection, but still under the cover of darkness. Very well. We shall be prepared for the trip."

Slocum saw how Beatrice pursed her bow-shaped lips, and he wanted to kiss them. But Ah So stood silently in the doorway, and he did not think it proper to kiss Beatrice. He touched the brim of his floppy black felt hat and left to find a proper carriage for the princess and her servant.

Slocum rested his hand on the butt of his Colt. Something wasn't right, and it gnawed at him like a dog chewing on a bone. Twisting in the hard carriage seat, he looked up and down the deserted alley for any sign of movement.

The mangy old cat he had seen the night before wasn't even prowling. The place was so lifeless he might have been in the middle of a desert—except a desert always crawled with life, if you knew where to look. Slocum had the uneasy feeling he wasn't looking in the right spots for the highbinders, and it would spell trouble later.

"John, here we are," came Beatrice's soft voice.

"Hurry and get inside," he said. He leaned over and pulled open the carriage door. Ah So ducked inside after Beatrice forced her to enter ahead of her. For a moment,

Slocum thought Beatrice was going to sit with Ah So, then she changed her mind and swung up to the seat beside him.

"This is too dangerous for you," he said. "Get inside where no one can see you."

"This will be all right, John. I rather like it," she said, snuggling closer. "The night will be a foggy one. I feel it in my bones."

He did, too. Banks of clouds moved across the bay, drifting ever lower until they touched the whitecaps kicked up by ocean current and soft breezes. But would a heavy fog hide Beatrice enough if the highbinders happened to see her beside him? Slocum didn't know and was loath to take the chance. More than one life rode on this.

There was Ah So to consider.

"I'd feel better if you were out of sight. Keep Ah So company."

"She is quite an independent lady, surprisingly so, considering her upbringing. Now, John, shall we be off? The sooner we start, the sooner we will arrive."

He saw it wouldn't do any good to argue. She had made up her mind, and he would only waste his time and breath. A sharp crack of the whip got the two-horse team moving. Slocum didn't want to push them too hard, preferring to keep their energy in reserve if he needed to outrun any pursuers, but as he drove down the winding roads threading about Nob Hill, he saw no one suspicious.

He saw no one, but still he had the feeling of being watched.

Slocum did not drive directly for the road south from San Francisco. Rather, he wound around in the city streets, waiting for the promised fog to roll in. He didn't have long to wait. Before he had driven five miles, the heavy mist thickened and cloaked the city streets until he could see no more than a few yards ahead.

Only then did he put the whip to the horses' rumps and

get them trotting faster. He took corners with reckless abandon, circling blocks and waiting for any who might follow, then racing down the straightaway to lose even the wiliest of pursuers.

The entire while, Beatrice held onto her hat and gasped with the sheer audacity of his driving. Only when they were in the country south of the city did she venture to speak.

"That is the most exciting carriage ride I've ever taken," she said. "I hope we can engage in other, even more exciting pursuits when we arrive in Oakland." Her hand crept to his leg. She squeezed gently, promising far more than Slocum cared to think about at the moment.

For all his maneuvers, his gut feeling told him they did not drive down the foggy road alone.

"Tell me where we're going in Oakland," he asked. "I'll drop the pair of you off and then return the carriage. With luck, I can get back before sundown tomorrow."

"So long?" She sighed. "I hoped you might spend the night."

"That's a mighty attractive offer and not one I'm going to turn down, but I have to get rid of the carriage. It might cause comment, unless there's a carriage house to hide it and the horses inside."

"There is not," Beatrice said. "This place is in the foothills. A friend who works at the Rescue Society owns it and has used it a few times for hiding others on the run from the authorities."

"So it might be known to the police?"

"No, of course not. I would never put Ah So at such risk!"

They drove for the better part of four hours through the fog and gloom, arriving at the house an hour before sunrise. Slocum helped Ah So from the carriage and Beatrice hurried her into the house, a much smaller dwelling than the one on Nob Hill, though this one seemed in better repair. Slocum considered staying the day, hoping no one took note of the carriage and two horses, then discarded the idea.

He wasn't one to think with his gonads. Staying would put them all at risk.

He still had the troublesome feeling that eyes fixed on him. Leaving the carriage, he went toward the house, but he quickly left the short path and dashed around to the rear of the house. From here, he cut across the next yard and came out in the street a hundred yards from where Beatrice and Ah So crouched behind shuttered windows.

Through the fog he saw a very tall man in a skintight suit. Then he was gone, leaving Slocum wondering if he had really seen anyone at all.

He might have been deceived by the shifting, swirling gray fog, but he didn't think so. William Considine had somehow tracked them to Oakland.

7

"Be sure who you let in," Slocum cautioned Beatrice Keller. He worried about leaving her and Ah So alone in Oakland since Considine obviously knew their location. After wrestling with the ins and outs of the situation, Slocum decided he could stop the danger to the women if he stopped William Considine.

That fit well with his own plans. Little Pete still owed him money, and Considine had dealings with the Gi Sin Seer leader. Slocum wasn't sure what those arrangements might be, but it hardly mattered to him. What concerned him most was Beatrice's safety and the money Little Pete had stolen by fixing the race.

"You worry so, John," Beatrice said, trying to keep it light, but the disquiet creeping into her voice told him she wouldn't sleep too well once he left. "Do you have to go? Right away?" Her hand rested warmly on his arm.

"The carriage ought to be returned to the sutler so there won't be any questions asked," he said lamely. There was so much more he wanted to do, but he didn't want to upset her more by telling her what it would be. She had a strong dislike for Considine already. Adding fuel to that served no purpose that Slocum could see.

"Go on, John, but hurry back. Please?" She turned her beautiful face up to him, her eyes half-closed. He could not resist kissing her on those perfect bow-shaped lips. The kiss lasted long, passionate seconds, then Beatrice crushed herself against his body, hugging him close. Slocum felt hot tears on his shirt where she buried her face. He held her for a moment, hand stroking over the falls of silky blonde hair. Then he pushed her away. If he didn't leave fast, he would stay. That might be the worst thing that could happen to all of them.

"I'll be back before you know it," he promised. With that, Slocum slipped out into the dense fog. Misty fingers stroked across his face and touched the wet spots on his shirt where Beatrice's tears had soaked in. Off in the distance he heard a mournful fog horn wailing and the soft ringing of a buoy bell. They were closer to the bay than he had thought for the sea sounds to be so loud.

He settled the nervous horses and started them back around the bay for distant San Francisco. He considered the ferry but doubted it would be running in such thick fog. As he drove the carriage, Slocum worried about an ambush set up by Considine. Every sound caused him to jump nervously, and by the time he reached San Francisco, he was drawn tighter than a bowstring and ready to explode.

After returning the carriage and horses, Slocum dickered a while to buy a new horse and gear. By the time he was satisfied with his purchase and the stabling fees, he had left very little of the money Beatrice had given him. He shrugged this off. He would collect the money due him from Little Pete soon enough. Slocum spent the day wandering the length of Dupont Gai between Pine and Bush Streets, entering the quaint bazaars and tiny shops filled with ivory and brass and odd assortments of trade goods. He scratched his head, wondering why the Chinese sold fireworks in butcher shops, fine porcelain in fish shops, jade in tea stores, or even elaborate seed-pearl headdresses in a small café where roast pig was prominently displayed for all passersby to see; but something more than this confusion of products for sale vied for his attention.

He had seen Lee Chuck collecting protection money from the merchants before. Now a pair of tough looking hatchet men did the dirty chore. One stood outside, arms crossed and hands hidden in voluminous sleeves. Slocum saw an occasional gleam from inside the sleeve and knew either knives or pistols were hidden there. Anything unusual would cause the highbinder to draw and start slashing or blazing away.

From all he had seen, the highbinders cared little who was in the way once they began killing.

The other highbinder entered the store and spoke rapidly in singsong Chinese to browbeat the storekeeper into paying. Slocum tried to guess how much these two extorted and failed. As before, he considered waylaying them and taking his money. They must work for Little Pete. But if they didn't, Slocum had no compunction against stealing from Little Pete's rival tong.

Slocum had to keep reminding himself there was more than his money at stake. He had to find Considine and stop him from bothering Beatrice. Perhaps Slocum could get the goods on Considine and force Henry Keller to get rid of his assistant. Slocum also wanted to find out what made Ah So such a sought-after target.

Walking slowly on the east side of the street, he trailed the two highbinders until they reached Bush and turned uphill to the west. He had spent the better part of the day watching them and now struggled to keep from losing them in the gloom of alleys away from the bright gaslights.

Slocum smiled when he saw the two men stop on a corner and wait impatiently. After ten minutes, a tall, well-built man strode up the street and went to them. Slocum would have recognized William Considine anywhere.

In the light of a gas lamp from far down the street, the puffy features of the man's rugged face were still immediately recognizable. Slocum touched the ebony handle of his Colt Navy and made sure the six-shooter rested easy. He figured he would need it soon enough.

Considine talked with the two highbinders and then held out his hand. He made an impatient gesture until the highbinder carrying the money reluctantly turned it over to the tall man. Slocum watched carefully how much the other Celestial wanted to use his weapons on Considine.

But he didn't. They bowed and backed off, then returned to Chinatown down the street where Slocum stood concealed in a doorway. The two passed within feet of Slocum without seeing him. He waited for them to disappear around the corner before he started after Considine.

Slocum's heart jumped to his throat. Considine had vanished again, as he had the night before into the Oakland fog. Then he heard the click click of the man's shoes against pavement. Slocum rushed forward and saw Considine striding down a side street as if he didn't have a care in the world. With all the money he had taken from the two Gi Sin Seer highbinders, Considine could afford to be mighty happy, Slocum thought.

"Little Pete," exulted Slocum, seeing Considine stop in a doorway. The well-dressed head of the tong stepped out and shoved more money into the tall man's hands. This took Slocum by surprise. He had expected Considine to be the courier for the money, giving the extortion over to Little Pete. He had no idea what went on, the tong boss giving Henry Keller's assistant money.

The two parted. Slocum considered following Little Pete. The Celestial had cheated him of the money at the racetrack, and Little Pete was more likely to know why the tongs sought Ah So as aggressively as they did. But William Considine had shuffled himself into the deck in such a way that Slocum decided to stick to him like fly-paper.

Considine headed north to the Barbary Coast again. The sound of the shooting galleries grew louder, as well as the hoarse cries from the bagnios and saloons filled with sailors. Considine might work for a wealthy man, but he had low tastes. Somehow, Slocum would have thought Considine would have felt more at home at the Union Club rather than a dive in the shadow of Telegraph Hill.

"Hey, mister, you look like a big one. Want what I can sell you?" A whore stepped out from a doorway and gyrated her hips.

Slocum ignored her and the crude comments she made about him when he passed her by without showing any interest. A few seconds later, she was propositioning another pedestrian. Picking up the pace, Slocum narrowed the distance between him and Considine. The time had come to collect what was owed him.

"Watch where yer goin'," bellowed an old salt. The sailor rolled from side to side, as if he still stood on a deck pitched by an ocean storm. Slocum stepped back and saw two others join the sailor. The man sounded drunk, but there was a clarity to his eyes that told the truth. He sought a fight.

Slocum spun to one side in time to avoid a slungshot from bashing in his head. Another seaman rushed forward, but Slocum was already responding. His fist crashed into the attacking seaman's face, breaking his nose and sending blood spattering in all directions. The mariner screeched and jerked away, banging into his friends.

The opportunity opened for Slocum to kick the man who had tried to bash in his brains. He followed with the barrel of his six-shooter on the top of the man's head, sending him facedown to the ground.

The cocking of the six-gun caused a sudden cessation of action. The sailor and his friends stared down the bore of Slocum's Colt Navy.

"Which of you wants to swallow the first lead pill?" Slocum shifted his aim from one to the next and then back to the sailor who had provoked the fight.

"You got us wrong, mister. We want to buy you a drink."

"Laced with knockout drops," Slocum said in disgust. The sailors had decided to make a few dollars by robbing whomever came along. They had chosen the wrong victim.

"No, no, you got it all wrong."

Slocum kicked the groaning man on the ground, then stepped over him, turning to keep his six-shooter leveled on the others.

"Get him out of here, or you'll go back to sea weighing a few bullets more than you do now."

The sailors grumbled but helped their companion to his feet. Together they lurched off, only to stop a block away and ready to work their ambush on a less alert, drunker dupe.

Slocum pressed close to a building and made sure no one followed him as he went to the corner, sure he had lost Considine. To his surprise, Considine stood in front of a large house decorated in fancy Queen Anne gingerbread. Slocum knew what business was conducted there. Women clad only in stockings and thin, filmy wraps sat on display inside, bare legs dangling over window ledges. A few bothered to call to men passing on the street. Most were too bored to try enticing customers to their beds.

Considine paced back and forth a few times, as if trying to make up his mind about entering. Before Slocum could reach him, Considine vaulted a low fence and strode up to the front door. He rapped twice. A black maid opened the door and ushered him inside.

Slocum let out a sigh of disgust. He might follow Considine into the whorehouse, but that created new problems. Slocum didn't want a dozen witnesses to

Considine's questioning. Worse, the brothel's bouncer would keep the peace or bust heads trying.

How long Considine might spend was a matter of concern for Slocum. Considine had a pocketful of money and might blow the entire poke on the women. Overpriced champagne and a half dozen eager Cyprians could steal away any size bankroll in an hour or less.

As he was tossed on the horns of his dilemma, Slocum saw a sea captain scuttling down the street from the opposite direction, his bandy legs pumping hard to make better time. The captain never slowed as he went to the front door. Slocum frowned when the door was opened, not by the maid but by William Considine.

The sea captain and Considine clearly knew each other by the way they shook hands. Henry Keller's right-hand man saw the captain inside and led him to the front room. Open windows drew Slocum, though he realized how dangerous spying on them might be.

Considine and the captain sat on facing chairs but bent forward so their heads were only inches apart. Talking in this fashion prevented their words from being heard even a few feet away. Slocum slunk away from the window, cursing his bad luck. What business did Considine have with this old salt?

What dealings did he have with Little Pete? He had bailed out the Celestial, so their business was of long standing. But Slocum understood none of it. Unanswered questions burned too brightly for him to walk away now. He hitched up his gun belt and went up the steps to the front door. He knocked twice, following Considine's lead. In less than a minute, the black maid opened the door.

"May I help you?" she asked, giving him a quick once-over.

"I'd like to avail myself of the services of one of your ladies," he said.

"Cain't do it this night. Come back t'morrow," she said, closing the door.

Slocum grabbed the door and held it open. "What's wrong? My money not good enough?"

"The whole house has been sold out for the night. Tomorrow, you come back 'morrow night and we fix you up jist fine."

Her insistent shoving forced Slocum to take his hand off the door. It closed with a click that irritated him more than anything else had in a long time. He couldn't even buy his way into a whorehouse. Stepping back, he looked along the front porch. These windows were closed. Only the one in the front parlor where Considine and the captain held their conference was open, save for those on the second floor where the whores showed off their fleshy wares.

He went back to the street, aware of eyes watching him. He walked away, then ducked into shrubbery and edged back to the window. Getting money and information from Considine proved harder than he had anticipated.

Inside, both the captain and Considine still talked. Now they had a sheaf of papers spread between them on a table. When a well-endowed woman entered the room, Considine placed his huge hands over the papers, then drew back.

"Clara, you decided to come keep us company."

"I'd never miss either you or Cap'n Jed. You're my best customers. The whole place is yours for the night, you and the captain." The woman perched on the arm of the chair where Considine sat and rested a hand on his shoulder.

"Get us some booze. I'm parched from all this talking, and I suspect the captain is, too."

"Right ye are, right ye are," piped up the seaman. "Talkin' all this business is thirsty work."

The madam laughed and went to a small bar at the side of the room. She poured four fingers of whiskey into water glasses and brought them back. The captain drained his in a gulp and held out the empty glass for more.

As the madam filled the glass again, Slocum worked to climb to a better vantage point. He peered down into the room at the papers on the table. They were legal documents, bills of sale or deeds, but more than this he could not tell.

"I'll supply you with fifty, if you can use them," Considine said.

"Fifty? I only got a clipper, not a battleship," laughed the captain. "But if you send me that many, I can take my pick of the litter."

"Agreed," Considine said. "That'll be—"

Slocum heard a twig break behind him. He turned and tried to whip out his Colt Navy. Heavy hands hammered into the backs of his legs, and he lost his balance. He fell heavily, still struggling to draw his six-shooter. A second blow crashed into the side of his head. The world spun in wild, crazy circles, but still he resisted.

A third and final blow pulled darkness down on him like a clinging, warm blanket.

8

Slocum awoke to rattling chains. He heaved to one side and was fetched up short. He struggled to no avail when the clanging increased and he felt biting pain in his ankles. His eyelids fluttered open and for a terrifying second, he thought he had gone blind. Then tiny slivers of pale light penetrated. He wasn't blind. He was in the dark hold of a ship.

His nose wrinkled at the heavy odors, and he felt the slow swaying of the ship as it rocked from side to side. Occasional groans from the hull told him they were still secured to a dock, but it hardly mattered. The fetters on his ankles were fastened to an iron ring driven into the planking. No matter how he tugged, he couldn't budge either the ring or the manacles.

"Don't go gettin' any fancy-ass ideas," advised a weathered sailor, dropping into the hold from a hatchway. "We nabbed you fair and square. You're gonna pull canvas with the best of 'em 'fore this journey's at an end."

"Where?"

"We're headin' to the Orient on the morning tide," the mate said, crouching just out of reach. His eyes danced as he looked from the manacles on Slocum's ankles to his face. He seemed amused at the anger smoldering inside Slocum. "I got myself shanghaied lo these many moons back. Took to the life at sea, I did. You will, too."

Slocum said nothing, trying to figure out how to get away. There was a padlock on the leg irons. That meant a key opened it. Where would it be kept?

"You one of them cow punchers? I seen your like before, but never talked to one. You ride horses and herd the beeves?"

"Where are you from?"

"Boston. Never set foot outside New England 'fore they recruited me. Truth was, I worked a bit on fishing boats, but no China clippers. Opened the world for me, surely it did."

"What's it worth for you to let me go free?"

The mate laughed uproariously at this. Tears ran down his suntanned cheeks and he held his sides as if they might split. He wiped his mouth and leaned back against the hull before he answered.

"There's not enough tea in China for that, laddy buck. Captain Craig'd have my head on the mast. Or keelhaul me. He likes to do that. You know what that means?" The mate tipped his head to one side when Slocum didn't answer. "They tie a rope to your feet and drag you completely under the ship, from starboard to larboard. Takes a strong man not to die right away."

"Hey, Jonesy, get that scum to work. We got a ton of crates to unload. Then there's the shipment headin' over to Shanghai."

"Righto," the mate agreed, getting to his feet. He reached into his wide sash and drew out a small, ugly-looking pistol. He held it casually so Slocum could see it.

"I kilt four men with this piece," Jonesy said. "I'm not hankerin' to kill another, but I will, if the need arises." He eyed Slocum, making it perfectly clear that Slocum would add a fifth notch to the small gun's handle if he got out of line.

"What do you want from me?"

"Work, laddy buck, work!" The mate laughed in glee. "You think it's work kickin' a horse's flanks and singin' to cows? We'll show you what *real* work is 'fore the tide sets us out to sea." He knelt and used a small key to unlock the shackles around Slocum's ankles. The mate backed away quickly before Slocum could get the circulation back into his legs to do more than stagger.

Motioning with the pistol, the mate got Slocum moving to the deck. The blast of fresh salt air caused Slocum to cough. It had been close below deck. He guessed he would be spending the rest of his life there if he didn't think of something fast.

Everywhere he looked, armed men herded others into lines moving heavy crates. It didn't take him too long to guess that well nigh a quarter of the ship's crew were, like him, being shanghaied. They shuffled about their work, heads down and looking as if they were going to die any second.

"What saloon did you get them from?" Slocum asked, indicating the others in the work detail.

The mate laughed again. "Several of them came from the Cobweb Palace. Old Meiggs gives them whatfor, then drops 'em through a trapdoor where we grab 'em. Trouble is, sometimes he puts too big a Mickey Finn in their drinks. Some don't ever wake up after that. But what a drunk it must be!"

Jonesy shoved Slocum toward the line of men struggling to get crates from the hold. After working fifteen minutes, Slocum's arms were aching and his back felt as if it would break. Each bale weighed close to two hundred pounds and, as best he could tell, these were nothing more than rags. As he worked, he kept an eye out for any chance to escape. The crewmen watching their prisoners gave nary a chance at flight. Slocum figured Captain Craig had promised keelhauling or worse to anyone letting one of his precious new crewmen get away.

"Keep your worthless backs bent to the task," bellowed a tall, bulky man dressed in a captain's uniform. He stood on the deck, a short whip in his hand. He applied the lash liberally to any he deemed slacking.

"Who's that?" asked Slocum of his nearest fellow shanghaied worker.

"Captain Craig. Cruel taskmaster, from all I heard."

"You look to be a sailor," Slocum said in surprise. "How'd you get into this pickle?"

The man shrugged. "Ships swap crew sometimes. I was on the good ship *Sarrantonio* and would have sailed again under Cap'n Albert, but I went into the wrong drinking emporium on me leave. These blackguards got me, they did."

"Silence!" bellowed Captain Craig. "Keep moving those bales. Look lively now. Fast. Get 'em to the dock fast as ye can!"

"What's so special about rags?" asked Slocum. All he got was a shrug from the shanghaied sailor, but Captain Craig came by and lashed him with the short whip. Slocum was driven to his knees. The pain across his shoulders made him grit his teeth and, for a moment, turned the world red with agony. He glared up at his tormentor.

"Keep workin' and no talkin'. I won't permit it on my crew." Captain Craig snapped the whip in front of Slocum's face. Slocum considered his chances of getting a grip around the man's throat and squeezing the life from his miserable body before the mate or others in the crew filled him with lead.

The odds were against him. Slocum would get his revenge later.

He struggled back to his feet and wrestled the bale of rags along the gangplank.

"That's better," the captain said, moving on. "Be quick about it. We don't have all night."

A trickle of blood from the wound ran down Slocum's back and soaked his shirt as he worked. He wasn't going to take this passively. As he struggled with the bale, he slowly pulled the innards from it. He thrust his hand deep into the bale and fished around. His fingers closed on a package wrapped in slick brown paper.

Slocum shoved a finger through the tough paper wrapping and pulled back. Sticky black tar on his finger confirmed what he had only suspected before. Captain Craig smuggled opium into San Francisco.

How Considine or Little Pete were mixed up in the scheme, Slocum couldn't say, but the raw opium had to be extremely profitable. The Chinese smoked tiny beads of it until they were completely docile, but Slocum knew white men were the biggest customers.

"Do you know Captain Jed?" Slocum called out to Jonesy.

"What are you yammerin' about?" demanded the mate. He looked uneasily in the direction of his captain as he came over to where Slocum leaned against the bale.

"Captain Jed," Slocum repeated. He described the man he had seen in the brothel swapping yarns with William Considine. "You know him?"

The mate looked as if he had swallowed a red-hot poker. His fingers worked nervously over the barrel of the small pistol.

"There are men along the Embarcadero you don't mess with. Captain Jed's one of 'em. You was prob'ly sold to Captain Craig by him. He's 'bout the biggest supplier of new crewmen in San Francisco."

"You mean he's the biggest shanghaier?"

"Get to work down there," barked the captain. "We have laundry to load when you have all that stacked."

Slocum started to tell the mate they smuggled opium from the Orient, then found himself beaten into a line to move huge hampers of laundry into the ship's hold to replace the bundles of rags laden with opium. The dried, condensed juice of the poppy was brought in and legitimate laundry taken back for cleaning. Both legs of the trip were profitable, though Slocum did not doubt the return from China garnered the ship's owner the most profit.

"Considine?" he muttered to himself. "Or Little Pete? Who owns this ship?"

"Jones, cut that man's tongue out if he says one more word," came Captain Craig's curt command to his mate. "I will tolerate no mouth from the crew."

"Aye, sir," the mate called up to his captain. Jonesy turned to Slocum and kicked him hard in the seat of the pants. "You heard 'im. You keep that pie hole of yours shut till we're at sea."

A cold shiver passed up Slocum's spine. *When they were at sea.* If the ship left the harbor and Slocum wasn't watching it from dry land, he was going to spend the next eight months pulling canvas sail and trying to keep from being keelhauled.

He hunkered down and pushed hard to get the bundle of laundry up the gangplank. As he strained, he shifted his weight to one side. The load went one way and he went the other, tumbling into the filthy water. Slocum hit hard and floundered a few seconds, thrashing about, then got his breath and barely saved himself from being crushed as the ship swung back on the waves and crashed into the dock.

Diving, he went to the bottom and tried to find his way away from the ship. But his air ran out too fast and he was forced to surface, sputtering and blowing water from his nose and mouth. When he looked up at the dock, he stared into no fewer than four six-shooters.

"Get back on dock," ordered the mate. "If you even look like you're going under again, I'll be double-damn sure you never take another breath of air." Jonesy's hand shook slightly as he sighted along the short barrel of his pistol. Slocum had no way to escape the mate or the others if they opened fire.

Still, for a brief instant, he considered dying then and

there rather than serving under Captain Craig as an impressed seaman.

He heaved himself out of the harbor and shook like a dog.

"Get him below decks and into irons," snapped the mate. "I don't want to see hide nor hair of him until we are out of sight of land."

"Wait, I can—" Slocum started forward and bumped into the mate. For a moment, they clung to one another, off balance. Jonesy yanked his gun far away to keep Slocum from grabbing it and caused both of them to crash to the dock.

"What's going on, Mr. Jones?" bellowed Captain Craig. "You are attracting attention. Get him out of sight! The harbor master is on his way to the ship!"

"Right away, sir," grunted the mate. He gave Slocum a swift kick in the ribs that doubled him over. Clutching his belly, Slocum lost all gumption to fight. Heavy hands dragged him up the gangplank and away from any hope for escape.

The heavy shackles snapped shut around his ankles again, and Slocum heard the crew returning to their work. From the progress they made, he knew it would not be long before the ship sailed. The tide was coming in and promised easy escape from San Francisco Bay. For Slocum, that would mean no escape at all.

He sat up and rubbed his legs. Then he looked around and saw no one. He fumbled in his pocket and pulled out the key to the shackles he had stolen from the mate when he stumbled into him. Jonesy had thought it was an attempt to get away. It had been, but Slocum saw that it was impossible to make a run from the dock without being shot. He needed his own six-shooter back, and he needed to be out of sight.

Two quick twists of the small key opened the locks. He stood and almost fell when the ship lurched under him. The rasping of canvas across wood and rope convinced

Slocum he had only a few minutes before the ship was at sea. He had watched the China clippers heading through the Golden Gate and out to sea but couldn't guess how long it took. He might have plenty of time—or only minutes.

Slocum stuck his head through the hatch and saw the crew occupied at their tasks. The captain stood on the deck, bellowing orders and snapping his short whip. Slocum boldly stood and walked to the small door leading to the area under the deck where the captain stood. Slocum ducked into the narrow passageway and immediately found the captain's quarters. It was the work of only seconds to find his belongings.

He grabbed his Colt Navy and strapped the holster around his waist. He was armed and ready to get off the ship now, even if he had to kill everyone standing in his way. Slocum doubted that would be necessary. Captain Craig would be inclined to obey the command to return to port with a six-shooter shoved into his ear.

Looking around, Slocum saw a small lockbox. He used a small metal bar to pry open the lock and grabbed a handful of greenbacks inside. It was small enough payment for all he had been through. With the money and his six-gun, he went back to the deck.

This time two of the crew spotted him when he poked his head out.

"One of the new crew. He's free!" cried a seaman.

This brought the captain and mate running. Slocum swung around, whipped out his Colt, and pointed it at the ship's master.

"Back to port. I want off!" Slocum ordered.

He expected the captain to obey. Instead, Captain Craig ducked and used the rolling of the deck to his advantage. Slocum found his six-shooter pointing at empty sky rather than the man's head. The pounding of bare feet against the deck told Slocum he had only seconds to act.

He spun around and fired. The first bullet hit one sailor

in the leg and knocked him off balance. The wounded salt slipped and fell facedown. The other sailor swarmed all over Slocum.

Wrestling, they slammed hard against the rail.

"Capture him," roared the captain. "Capture him and then give him twenty lashes of the cat-o'-nine-tails!"

Slocum tried to use his pistol barrel against the sailor grappling with him but couldn't. He got his knees up and forced the man away. A hard kick sent the seaman stumbling into three others. With an agile twist, Slocum got to the railing. He froze when he looked out and saw nothing but slow-moving waves on gunmetal gray ocean.

"Take him!" shouted the captain.

Slocum dived overboard. He hit the cold water and seemed to be swallowed by endless sea. Finally fighting back to the surface, he came up, sputtering. The ship had moved on smartly, heading toward the Orient. Men on the deck pointed and one even fired a shot in his direction, but the distance was too great.

Slocum found he still gripped his Colt. Floating on his back, Slocum shoved the six-gun into his holster and fastened the keeper over the hammer to keep it from falling out. Then he kicked free of his boots. Keeping his Colt was a risk, but he felt better, even with it dragging him down.

He started swimming for a distant patch of fog, not sure where dry land and safety lay.

9

Slocum had no idea where land lay. He simply kept paddling toward the distant fogbank because in any other direction lay only limitless ocean. He did not remember there being any fog while he toiled to unload the rags with the opium hidden among them or when he had pushed the laundry carts into the hold, but he did not know exactly how long it had taken him to get free of the leg irons or to sneak into the captain's cabin to retrieve his Colt. Minutes? Was that long enough for fog to form?

He had counted on the ship not being under way long enough to get out of sight of land.

As he swam, he became aware of fins breaking the choppy water in front of him. Increasingly worried, he swam faster and tired out sooner. The fins came closer with an ominous determination. He tried to remember everything he had heard of sharks. All he knew was that they ate anything that moved and that their main breeding ground was in Bodega Bay north of San Francisco. Needing a rest but fearing to do so, Slocum floated motionlessly in the water, his feet under him. The downward tug of his gun in his cross-draw holster told him he ought to drop it. A few less pounds might mean the difference between life and death. But he refused to abandon his six-shooter.

With the first fin came another, circling warily, as if unsure what this new denizen of the ocean might be. Friend? Dinner? Or did it matter to a shark?

The fins moved closer, like wolves sniffing out their prey. Then they swam away and vanished beneath the surface. Slocum knew he was not safe. These predators worked like birds of prey, as comfortable going up and down in their environment as they were going back and forth. Even now they might be racing toward the surface from far below him, ready to take a single snap that would cut him in half.

Still tired but knowing he could not swim much longer, Slocum paddled again for the fog. If he was going to be eaten, he would die attempting to reach dry land and not simply die without a struggle. After what seemed hours, the first tendrils of fog touched his face as he lifted it from the water to greedily suck in air. A thrill of panic surged through him when he realized he might easily swim in circles now that all reference had vanished into the gray mist. He rolled onto his back and floated, listening hard.

A buoy bell rang in the distance. He tried to locate it but couldn't. He was too tired, too confused. It might have been better if he had remained on the ship and gone to China.

As this thought crossed his mind, Slocum snapped alert. Anger burned brighter, and he knew it was better dying for his freedom than living in slavery aboard the China clipper under the cruel captain's lash. His legs scissored harder, and he shot forward. How long he swam, he did not know, but a sudden sharp pain in his arm caused him to flounder.

Blood gushed from the cut on his forearm. He thought a shark had attacked. Then he worried a shark would attack. They smelled blood as easily as a bloodhound tracking through the woods. After a few seconds of panic, Slocum came to realize something had changed. When he cut his arm, his feet had come up under him and now rested on solid ground. He stood neck-deep in water—but it was solid under his bare feet.

"Land," he gasped out, working up the gentle slope hidden by the waves. He fell forward onto a rocky beach and lay there gasping for breath, the surf coming after him and trying to reclaim his body for the hungry sea.

He resisted and refused to yield that easily. Slocum dug his fingers into the sand and pulled himself forward until he was entirely out of the water. Only then did he roll over and sit up. He couldn't see more than five yards through the patch of fog, but he definitely had come ashore. It took more than ten minutes for his strength to come back. Tending the cut on his arm from the submerged rock passed the time until he could climb the steep cliff above him.

An hour passed as he made his way up the face of the rocky precipice. He sat on the edge of the cliff and stared downward at the fifty-yard distance he had struggled up. Then he heard the jangle of harness and the neighing of horses. A carriage passed not ten feet away, the driver staring at him as if he was a drowned rat washed up on the shore.

Slocum had to laugh. He *was* a drowned rat. Without boots. But he still carried his Colt Navy and the water-logged wad of greenbacks he had stolen from the captain's lockbox. Slocum took out the scrip and squeezed it dry of water, laying the bills out in the sun poking through the fog.

When the sun finally showed and he got a better idea of the time, he was amazed that it could hardly be ten o'clock. He had been aboard the ship moving the contraband and then heading out to sea and swimming back for a lifetime. Longer.

He found walking difficult on the sharp gravel in the

roadway. Moving to the shoulder proved little better. The saw-edged grass tore at his feet and made walking difficult. Going in the direction taken by the carriage seemed the wisest course. It had to lead back to San Francisco or at least some small outpost of civilization where he could use a few of his hard-won greenbacks to buy a new pair of boots.

"Beatrice," he muttered. Through all his troubles, he had forgotten about her and Ah So. William Considine knew where they hid—and William Considine had shanghaied him. Slocum didn't know what Henry Keller's assistant was mixed up in, but it looked to be opium smuggling, shanghaiing, and dealing with Little Pete in extortion and blackmailing. He might even have a hand in the horse race fixing. The more Slocum learned, the more he realized that Considine was involved in everything illegal in San Francisco.

Slocum picked up the pace, but his feet began to bleed. Hobbling along, he finally found a house set off the road. He knocked on the door and a servant opened.

"What do you want?" the woman asked coldly. Slocum explained and was shown around back, where he sat on the back stoop. The housekeeper brought him warm water, soap, and bandages.

"You can ride into town with the grocery boy. He's late, as usual," she complained.

"Much obliged," Slocum said. "Can I pay you for this?"

The woman sniffed indignantly. "Get yourself boots and new clothes. And a bath." With that, she closed the kitchen door and let Slocum stew until the tow-headed boy came driving up with the wagon loaded with supplies for the woman's kitchen. In exchange for the ride back to San Francisco, Slocum unloaded the wagon.

Dropped off near a mercantile, Slocum found clothing and boots but decided to get back to Beatrice Keller before worrying about a bath. He smelled like seaweed and had oozing wounds on both feet and his arm, but he thought he could ride. He went to the stable and paid the stableboy for tending the piebald. Slocum headed south, ready to round the bay and get back north to Oakland and Beatrice but soon found it almost impossible to ride.

Dizziness assailed him, and he wobbled in the saddle. He clung to the pommel and kept the horse walking steadily. Slocum was not quite sure how long it took to reach Oakland. The entire day passed in a daze, and he was hardly able to recognize the house where Beatrice had holed up with Ah So.

"Beatrice?" he called, knocking on the door. The effort almost cost him consciousness. To Slocum, the rapping came out loud. It took a supreme act of will for him to realize he had been weakly scratching and nothing more. The door opened, Beatrice gasping at the sight dumped on her doorstep.

"Ah So! Help me. Hurry!"

"Hello," Slocum said. "I told you I'd come back." He wanted to say more, but he passed out.

Sunlight slanting through the window made him sneeze. He rolled over, then came instantly awake. He lay between crisp white sheets in a soft bed. Slocum pushed the sheets back and sat up, looking around the tiny room. Like the house on Nob Hill, this one was dusty and had protective cloths tossed over the unused furniture. The far window had the curtains pulled back to let in the bright sun, and he had a sense of someone else in the house.

His clothing had been hung on a straight-backed chair beside the bed. He drew his six-shooter, then saw it needed oiling and cleaning. The dip in the ocean had not done it any good. Feeling better with the six-gun in hand, though, Slocum padded on cat's feet to the door and looked into the next room.

"Beatrice," he said. The lovely blonde looked up, startled.

"John! I hadn't expected you to be up and around so quickly."

"Was I only asleep a couple hours?" he asked, laughing.

"Two days," she corrected. "You stumbled in here and passed out. What happened to you? I was so worried when you didn't come right back."

For the first time Slocum realized he was bare-ass naked. He quickly returned to the bedroom where he climbed into his pants. Again, dizziness hit him like a sledgehammer, forcing him to remain seated. When he recovered a mite, Beatrice was in the doorway staring at him.

"You need food. I wasn't able to get you to take more than broth."

"I am hungry enough to eat a horse," he said. As if to emphasize his point, his belly rumbled like a foghorn.

"A horse as big as Heavy Seas?" she said, chuckling. "After that race, Papa might be willing to sell him to a butcher."

"Even Heavy Seas," Slocum said. "Anything but hardtack." He shuddered at how close he had come to living off hardtack and maggoty meat for the next eight months of his life.

"Rest while I get some food. Then you can tell me what happened to you."

Slocum made his way to the kitchen and sat heavily at a rickety table. Beatrice bustled about, fixing this and that, nothing too elaborate but nothing Slocum was going to turn his nose up at. He followed the mountain of food with two glasses of fresh water.

"Anything but saltwater," he said. "I drank enough of that to last me the rest of my life."

"What went on?"

Slocum outlined all that had happened, then asked, "How likely is it that Considine is using your father's position to further his own fortunes?"

"Possible," Beatrice said slowly. She pushed a strand of blonde hair from her eyes. The way the sunlight gleamed on her hair made it seem she wore a halo of the purest spun gold. Slocum found it hard to concentrate on learning more about Considine when presented with such a lovely picture.

"I've seen him engage in some of the worst crimes around. The opium dealing probably brings him the most money, but he bailed Little Pete out of jail just before you got me," Slocum said.

Beatrice shivered. "I had no idea he was involved in so much illegal activity. Just speaking to that loathsome Little Pete ought to be enough to have Papa fire him."

Slocum started to speak, then bit his lip. One of the first things he had heard about Little Pete and his tong, the Gi Sin Seer, was that it blackmailed people. If Considine was involved with the tong, he might be blackmailing Henry Keller. Slocum had no idea what dark secrets Keller might want to hide, but a man of his standing in the community might want to hide a great deal.

Even if Henry Keller's secrets were trivial, it might cause a black spot on his reputation that would reflect poorly on his daughter. In spite of what Beatrice said about her father, Slocum thought Henry Keller would do about anything to protect her.

"It won't do any good taking this to the San Francisco police," Slocum said. "I don't have hard evidence, and he might be paying off most of them. Considine's influence might even extend all the way to the judges. I've never heard anyone call them honest."

Beatrice laughed, but it carried derision rather than humor. "The *Alta California* repeatedly reveals how corrupt the judges are. News reports do little good—except when the Regulators march."

"Vigilantes?" It was Slocum's turn to shiver. He didn't cotton much to citizens taking the law into their own hands. They usually hanged a few people, guilty or not hardly mattered, and then figured they had cleaned up the outlaw element in their community. More often than not, the biggest crooks were the ones leading the necktie party.

"I heard tell of a bunch called the Hounds," Slocum said.

"Terrible criminals," agreed Beatrice.

"They became the Regulators. Criminals putting others in jail or stringing them up." Slocum wanted no part of it.

"Something had to be done," Beatrice said almost plaintively. "John, why do you go on like this? I don't want to talk about it."

"Even if Considine might be coming after Ah So?" Slocum leaned back. His belly was full and his injuries bandaged and on the mend, but he found it almost impossible to keep his eyelids open. He hoisted himself from the table and went into the parlor and sat on the hard couch. A spring poked him in the back, but he hardly noticed. He was slowly drifting back to sleep.

"He would have nothing to do with that, I think," Beatrice said, but her tone convinced Slocum she wasn't really sure.

"Tell me about Ah So," he said.

"She came in on a ship about a month ago," Beatrice said. Slocum leaned back and listened with half an ear. This was important. Beatrice finally told him something important about the Chinese girl, but it was so difficult to stay alert. "She joined the Hook Took juggling troupe because she seemed to have no real talents. It was soon after that people started trying to kidnap her."

"What people?" asked Slocum. But he never heard the answer. He succumbed to exhaustion and soon snored loudly on the parlor couch.

10

Slocum awoke to darkness. He reached for his six-shooter and found it on the couch beside him. He pushed himself straighter and found he had been covered by a thin blanket.

"Beatrice?" he called. Something wasn't right. He listened hard but heard no movement in the house. "Beatrice!" he called louder. Slocum got to his feet and went into the bedroom. He quickly dressed, pulling on his new boots. They creaked and pinched at his feet, but they were better than walking on the cuts and bruises he had gotten from his hike into San Francisco.

He slipped out the bedroom window and went scouting. He circled the house and came upon his piebald horse tethered out back. It cropped contentedly at thick grass and weeds. It needed currying, but that could wait. With every step he took, he felt something awful was about to happen.

He spun, six-shooter out and cocking at the sound on the porch. He came out of the gunfighter's crouch when he saw Beatrice standing there, wringing her hands.

"What's wrong?" he demanded.

"It's Ah So. She hasn't returned. I sent her to the mar-

85

ket. I didn't think there would be any problem. That was almost four hours ago.''

Slocum cursed under his breath. It was crazy to send the Chinese girl out on an errand when Considine knew where they hid—but Slocum hadn't told Beatrice that. There had not been time, and he had been too exhausted in the aftermath of the shanghaiing.

''When did she go?''

''A few minutes before you woke up the first time,'' Beatrice said. ''She'd been gone only minutes. Ten at the most when you ate.''

Slocum had been in such a bad way from lack of food and sleep he hadn't noticed Ah So's absence.

''It's been four hours since I fell asleep in the parlor?'' This wasn't as much a question as it was a statement to fix details in his mind. In four hours every tong in San Francisco could have whisked Ah So away and gotten halfway to China. He tried to remember some of the details Beatrice had told him of the Chinese girl's arrival, but it was all hazy.

Details didn't matter now. What mattered was getting her back safely.

''Which market did you send her to?''

''Why, the farmers' market down the road. I thought to go find her myself, but I am so cowardly, John! I couldn't do it. And I wanted to wake you, but was afraid to do that, too. Nothing seemed the right course of action.''

Slocum pushed this aside. Beatrice had panicked and then had frozen like a deer with a lantern turned on it. He went to sit on the porch at her feet. He began working on his Colt. The mechanism was in need of cleaning and oiling from the drenching it had taken in the Pacific. He expertly wiped down the pieces, then reassembled the six-shooter, knowing oil would have to wait. He dry-fired it a few times, then loaded it.

"Will that be necessary?" Beatrice asked, a catch in her voice.

"Can't rightly say, but is there any reason for Ah So not to come straight back after buying her vegetables?"

Beatrice shook her head, sending a thin halo of blonde hair in all directions. She ran a trembling hand through the disarray, then bit her lower lip in frustration.

"I should have awakened you, but I don't know. Or I might have asked Papa for help. He's not too keen on aiding the Chinese, but he would do it for me, I think, if I begged enough."

"Let's get to the market. Keep your eye out for her. Ah So might have been waylaid in some other way."

"You mean a broken leg or helping someone?"

"I don't know what I mean," Slocum declared. He swung into the saddle and helped Beatrice up behind. The horse snorted at such an outrageous weight and then moved slowly in the direction Slocum wanted. They rode down the road toward the nearest knot of buildings. Many were deserted, and the few that were inhabited were falling apart from neglect.

The closer they came to the middle of Oakland, the more people and businesses they encountered. But at the market where Ah So was most likely to have gone, they found no trace of the young woman. Slocum dropped to the ground and said to Beatrice, "Stay here. I'll be right back."

He went into the market and found the proprietor.

"What can I do for you, mister?" the storekeeper asked. "Got some nice apples. And grapes. They grow like weeds up north. Good eating."

"A Chinese girl," Slocum said. He saw the man's expression change. Like so many proprietors, he didn't cotton much to having Celestials in his store. "She came in to buy some vegetables. Maybe even some of those fine grapes you were going on about."

"Ain't seen no one," the man said sullenly.

"No one?" Slocum took a few of the dried greenbacks from his pocket and laid them atop a crate of melons. "Maybe you took pity on this poor Chinese girl and gave her some of the rotted produce." He added another bill to the pile. The shopkeeper's greed was getting the better of him. A final greenback settled the matter.

"She came in well nigh three hours back. I sold her a few things, but don't you go tellin' anyone about that."

Slocum shook his head. He wanted to gut-shoot the son of a bitch, but he held his temper.

"See anything unusual? Like men following her?"

"There were a couple. I didn't pay them no nevermind. They stood outside and faded away like a shadow in the bright sunlight when she left."

"She head south when she left?"

"Nope, she went west, straight for the harbor. That I remember 'cuz she was hurrying along. She moseyed in, but she ran out."

Slocum pivoted on his heel and left. Beatrice sat uneasily astride the horse, waiting to hear what Slocum had found out.

"She went west," Slocum said. "You know anyone in that direction?"

"No, John, no one. And I am sure Ah So doesn't, either. Why wouldn't she return to the house?"

"She was being followed," Slocum said, putting his heels to the horse's flanks. The piebald pony took off at a trot. Slocum's head swiveled from side to side for any sign of Ah So, but it was Beatrice who first spotted the highbinders. She gripped his arm and dug her fingernails into his flesh.

"John, look," she whispered in fright.

He wheeled the horse around and took a trail away from the tight knot of ramshackle houses ahead. When he was out of sight down the street, he dismounted.

"I don't know what's going on. You stay here and wait for me to come back."

"What if you don't come back?" Beatrice asked in a choked voice.

"Go find your pa and tell him what's going on. Tell him everything, including everything I've told you about Considine."

"John, let's get the police. Let them handle this."

Slocum snorted in disgust. He squeezed her hand when she reached for him, then set out back along the street he had just ridden until he found the first of the hatchet men. Four of them crouched in shadows, intent on a single empty house. Slocum knew better than to tangle with so many of the highbinders. They would carve him like a Christmas goose unless he could plug all four of them before their confederates rushed him.

Slocum wasn't going to take a risk like that, even with his trusty Colt working perfectly.

Keeping low and moving like a shadow over velvet, Slocum circled the house. He found eight more highbinders waiting, but these were as interested in the first group of four as they were in the house and its contents. He continued to scout and finally returned to where Beatrice anxiously waited for him. She rushed forward, threw her arms around his neck and hugged him tightly.

"John, you're back. Where's Ah So?"

"I think she's in the deserted house. She's staying low, but I saw movement inside."

"The tong hatchetmen," protested Beatrice. "They should have captured her by now, if they'd wanted."

"That's the part I don't quite understand. It's as if they—" A light dawned and Slocum knew what was happening. He grabbed Beatrice by the arms and looked squarely at her. "There's not one gang of highbinders trying to kidnap her, there are *two*."

"Two? Little Pete's Gi Sin Seer and the Bo Sin Seer?"

"Might be. I think this goes farther than a squabble over who gets to call the shots in Chinatown. Both sides want Ah So, but neither can make the first move without the other stabbing them in the back."

"What are we going to do?"

Slocum grinned. "While the two of them fight over her, we'll grab her and get Ah So out of there," he said with more confidence than good sense. Still, the sheer audacity of the plan appealed to him.

"What do you want me to do?"

"You'll have to cause a diversion so I can sneak inside and get Ah So out the back way. There are two small bands in the rear, only four or so. I can set them to fighting one another, but the rest . . . the rest you have to distract long enough for us to get away."

Slocum saw the set to Beatrice's jaw and knew he could depend on her. He quickly outlined what he wanted her to do, then set off on foot again to find the rear entrance to the house.

Slocum waited impatiently for the ruckus Beatrice was supposed to create. On his left, hidden in a tall stand of weeds, lay two highbinders. To his right, melting in the shadows of an outhouse were another pair, these two standing with hatchets in their hands, waiting to attack.

Slocum decided to give them the chance they sought. He carefully judged distances, then cut loose, sending a pair of bullets ripping through the flimsy wood of the outhouse. This produced exactly the result he had hoped it would.

Both hatchetmen rushed out, waving their weapons high over their heads. Slocum flushed the other two from the weeds with three well-placed shots. They leaped to their feet and shrieked with a blood lust that momentarily froze Slocum.

Then the four crashed together like some elemental force of nature. Hatchets flashed in the dim light of a thousand stars and knives drove for exposed bellies. Slocum sprinted straight for the back door of the house and burst inside, breathless. Ah So huddled in one corner of the room, a basket of vegetables at her feet.

"Come on," he said. "We've got to get out of here!"

Ah So did not move.

"Damnation," Slocum said. He bent over and tried to get her to stand. She shied away like a frightened fawn. He saw he could never get her to run out. Reloading, he thought furiously of other ways out of this trap. There didn't seem to be any. Ah So had to cooperate—or die.

"You're going to be kidnapped," he said carefully, "if you don't come with me. Miss Keller is outside." Even as he spoke, he heard the hard pounding of a horse's hooves in the street. Beatrice launched her all-out frontal assault to throw confusion into the ranks of highbinders.

"Missy Keller?" Ah So stood and peered out, her ebony eyes wide.

"That's her. She's risking her life to get you out of here. We have to go *now*," insisted Slocum. He grabbed Ah So's arm and dragged her toward the back door. Then he froze. The battle in the back had ended sooner than he had anticipated. The two holding hatchets stood over the bodies of their fallen foes.

Slocum leveled his Colt Navy and fired as accurately as he could. He winged one highbinder but the other dived for cover, yelping in his singsong tongue for help. Unfortunately for Slocum and Ah So, reinforcements came running fast.

A new flurry of fighting occurred between the highbinders, but it subsided. Slocum wasn't sure if one side won out over the other or if they simply quieted down to figure out what was going on.

"Is there any other way out of here?" he asked Ah So. She simply stared at him, not speaking. He cursed and rushed to the front of the house to see what effect Beatrice's diversion was having.

The blonde had ridden hell-bent for leather through the center of the highbinders, but they had not scattered or even been all that confused by her headlong hectoring.

Slocum saw one highbinder reach out to grab the bridle of the piebald horse. Slocum snapped off a shot, then followed it with three more accurate slugs. One caught the hatchet man in the side of the head and sent him crashing to the street.

"Get out of here!" shouted Slocum.

"Do you have her?"

"Ride!" he bellowed, wishing Beatrice wasn't so hard-headed. He emptied his six-shooter in the direction of another Celestial intent on grabbing Beatrice and dragging her from the saddle. One bullet caught the highbinder in the leg and caused him to sit down heavily, but reloading took precious long seconds and allowed the tong killers to surge forward again.

Beatrice put her heels into the horse's flanks and it reared, striking out with its forelegs. One hoof caught a hatchet man in the face and sent him spinning. The others skidded to a halt and began to circle, to pull Beatrice from her seat. She cheated them of her capture. Beatrice sent the piebald horse jumping forward, over the low fence circling the house's yard and toward the front porch.

The horse crashed through the rotted wood and shied, but the piebald somehow managed make its way into the front room, knocking Beatrice from the saddle.

Slocum rushed to her side and fired into the mass of highbinders running to capture her. He winged one and scattered the rest. It gave him a passing pleasure to see two of the men locked in combat, each trying to gut the other. Cradling her head in his lap, Slocum heaved and got a dazed Beatrice sitting up.

"Inside, help her get inside," Slocum urged Ah So. The Chinese girl scuttled forward and dragged Beatrice to safety, such as it was. Bullet holes began appearing in the thin, rotted walls as the highbinders settled their disputes among themselves and turned their attention to the trio inside the house.

"What happened, John?" Beatrice rubbed her forehead. A nasty welt ran from one side of her forehead to the other where she had banged herself on the door lintel as the horse bolted. She struggled to get away from the nervous horse, who was trapped in the small room. Slocum held her close to keep her from standing. More and more lead flew through the walls, turning it to splinters.

"Your routing technique wasn't as successful as it might have been," Slocum said. "We're in the house, but at least all three of us are in this together now."

"Ah So!" Beatrice saw the Chinese girl for the first time.

Ah So knelt down and began rattling endlessly in her singsong language.

"Wait, slow down, I understand so little Chinese," said Beatrice.

"What's she saying?" asked Slocum, reloading again. He was running low on ammunition. They would have to get out of there fast, or the highbinders would overwhelm them by sheer numbers. A single all-out rush would be all it would take.

"I can't follow too much of it. Something about a pearl. The emperor's pearl."

"Do you think she stole a pearl belonging to the Chinese emperor?"

"It's possible. She's so excited, and my knowledge of her language is limited." To the girl, Beatrice said, "Calm down. Slow. Very slow."

Ah So nodded and repeated what she had said.

"All I get is the 'emperor's pearl,' repeated over and over. She might know where it is. Is that true? You know where this pearl is?"

Ah So rattled off more until Beatrice stopped her.

"She knows where the pearl is, but I'm getting confused about what she is saying about it. Here in San Francisco, but there's something more I cannot—"

The creaking of flooring alerted Slocum to the attack. He swung around and fired at a highbinder coming at them from the direction of a bedroom. But even as he killed this Chinese assassin, two more rushed forward, brandishing their hatchets. He fired and caused them to veer to one side. One crashed into Ah So and grappled with her.

The piebald horse got spooked and kicked, taking care of the second tong killer. Slocum heard other movement on the front porch and out back.

Spinning toward the rear of the house, he got off a pair of shots that made one highbinder duck. Then he heard Beatrice scream. Turning to aid her, he saw two Celestials holding her, keeping her from defending herself by pinning her arms to her sides. A third highbinder slugged her.

Slocum shot him in the back.

And then something heavy crashed into the back of Slocum's neck. He fought to keep on his feet. Sharp pain exploded in Slocum's head. He triggered a round that went into the flooring, and then he crashed down, darkness swallowing him completely.

11

Slocum coughed and rolled to one side, wondering what caused the liquid in his face. He reached up, mind still blurred from pain. He touched something sticky. Coming to slowly, he held his hand away and saw blood. His own blood. This brought him up fast. Memory returned in a flood.

"Beatrice!" he called. No answer. "Ah So!" He rolled again and tried to find his Colt Navy. The six-shooter had fallen to the dusty floor. It took several seconds for him to retrieve his side arm and cock it. He tried to remember if he had emptied the cylinder firing at the highbinders and found he could not.

His vision cleared, and he saw it was pitch dark in the house. He used a wall as a support to stand, then he explored the house. For a place that had been the center of a frantic firestorm of bullets earlier, it was now silent as a grave.

Slocum winced as he touched the bleeding spot on the back of his head. A hatchet had laid his skull open, but somehow he had avoided being killed. The flood of blood from the wound must have convinced his attackers he had

95

died then and there. Otherwise, they would have finished the job they had started.

"They *did* finish their job," Slocum allowed after completing his inspection of the house. Both women were gone, and with them any trace of the men who had kidnapped them. Try as he might, Slocum could not even locate a body. The highbinders had taken all their dead with them, leaving behind only small traces of evidence, certainly nothing that would interest the Oakland police enough to search for Beatrice.

Sitting out front, Slocum considered what he could do to find Beatrice and get her back. Ah So had said she knew where a fabulous pearl stolen from the Chinese emperor was hidden. For all Slocum knew, she might be the thief and had fled the country, coming to San Francisco and hiding the pearl. He tried to envision what this pearl must be like. He had seen some amazing ones in his day, both white and black. For an emperor to order the tongs to find it, if such were even possible, meant incredible wealth.

Slocum's mood darkened as he realized how little he really knew of what was going on. Ah So had stolen a treasure and come to San Francisco, then the Gi Sin Seer and Bo Sin Seer had tried to capture her. Finding anyone in Chinatown willing to even speak to him would be a fool's errand, Slocum knew. He had tried earlier and found nothing but blank stares or outright fear as he questioned merchants about William Considine. Getting any reply if he asked about a tong or Little Pete or Ah So's whereabouts would be worse than banging his head against a wall.

The police were no help. He couldn't hope to find Beatrice Keller on his own. That left him only one resource. He pushed to his feet and went around to the back of the house where the piebald horse nervously cropped at the weeds. How the horse had gotten free of the house uninjured, he neither knew nor cared. It had, and it provided transportation.

Slocum mounted and began a long ride.

"Tell him his daughter is a goner if he doesn't see me," Slocum said loudly. He wanted his voice to carry past the meddling butler and through the house so Henry Keller could hear. "She's been kidnapped, and I know how to get her back, but I need help."

"Sir, Mr. Keller is a busy man. He has no time for—"

"She was kidnapped along with Ah So, the Chinese girl she was trying to help through her Rescue Society."

The butler tried to close the door, but Slocum saw his loud statements had flushed his quarry. Down the long corridor leading from the door came Henry Keller, walking like royalty ascending his throne.

"That's all right, Charles," Keller said. "I will see the gentleman."

"Gentleman," scoffed the butler, barely loud enough for Slocum to hear. The butler stepped aside and allowed Slocum in, his expression implying that he would have to clean the floors after such an unwanted visitor left.

"What's this nonsense about Beatrice?" Keller said.

Slocum explained quickly all that had happened. He watched Keller's smug, self-assured expression begin to fade, then melt into outright fear.

"The tong has her?"

"I assume so. Perhaps the one led by Little Pete, perhaps a rival. I don't know, and there's no way I can find out."

"But how would I know?"

"I've poked around San Francisco enough to know the police are in your pocket. Ask them to find out. You pay them enough."

Keller shook his head. His face turned even redder than

normal, as if he might keel over at any instant. Slocum decided to keep applying pressure to the man. He was Beatrice's only hope.

"Considine might know."

"William? Why would he know anything about this? What are you saying?"

"He bailed Little Pete out of jail, he has dealings with the Gi Sin Seer tong, and he certainly knows his way around Chinatown. I've seen him up and down Dupont Gai talking real chummy with many of the highbinders."

"William? But that's not possible. He doesn't—"

"I almost got shanghaied. I think Considine is engaged in selling slaves to the captains of the clipper ships, as well as being involved in opium smuggling."

Keller went into his study and sank into a huge chair. As large as it was, his bulk still dwarfed it. He shook his head slowly.

"How long have you been digging into all this?" Keller finally asked.

"A few days. Since after Little Pete and his henchman fixed the horse race, causing Heavy Seas to lose. I think Considine was involved in that, too. He bet against Heavy Seas, knowing the horse was going to lose."

"What?" Keller's eyes widened, then narrowed, as if Slocum had finally touched on something truly reprehensible. "He was rigging the races so *my* horse would lose?"

"He had a powerful lot of money in his pocket after the race."

"I shall dismiss William immediately. No, I'll do worse than that. He will rue the day he ever crossed Henry Keller!"

"Don't do that. If you do anything to spook him, you might never find Beatrice."

"I warned her about that Rescue Society of hers. I knew it would only lead to trouble. She spent so much money on it, and now this. Horrible, absolutely horrible!"

"Charles!" Keller shouted. "Bring the carriage around. Mr. Slocum and I are going to see Chief Gordon right away."

Slocum was uneasy sitting in the San Francisco police chief's office just off Portsmouth Square. He fidgeted and shifted his weight in the chair while Keller spoke with the officer. It was almost a relief when Keller waved imperiously, summoning him into the chief's office. It was obvious who was in charge.

"Mr. Slocum is sure my daughter has been taken to some unknown spot in Chinatown. How long will it take to find her?"

"It might be helpful to hunt for Ah So, also," Slocum said. "The two of them are probably being held together, and it is the Chinese girl the tong is interested in. Miss Keller is only a captive because of her interest in Ah So."

"Chinatown," mused the police chief. He shook his bald head and light shone off the bright pink patch of skin. "There's not much we can do down there. Specials patrol there, mostly. The few of my boys walking the beat down there have an unhappy time of it. No one talks to 'em, and there is little chance of findin' out anything by chance."

"You're saying you can't find Beatrice Keller or Ah So?" Somehow, Slocum was not unduly surprised. Chinatown was closed to anyone not from the Orient. Anyone other than William Considine.

"If we searched door to door, there is no chance of findin' her. She could be moved from spot to spot in their damned underground tunnels."

"Tunnels?"

"The entire city under Chinatown is riddled with 'em. They burrow like moles, diggin' down and expanding so they can have their filthy opium dens where we can never find 'em."

"That's a bleak picture, Chief," Slocum said. "What are your chances of finding William Considine?"

"Ah, now, in that there might be some hope. From what Mr. Keller here says, this Considine fella haunts the shooting galleries in the Barbary Coast. Anything in the shadow of Telegraph Hill is fair game, and we have informants aplenty there."

"But?" Slocum read the hesitation in Chief Gordon's voice.

"But it takes time. We cannot expect a patrol to come in brimmin' over with news of your Mr. Considine."

Slocum watched Henry Keller's expression as the chief signed Beatrice Keller's death certificate. He couldn't read what the play of emotions meant. Keller was not the kind of man to accept this kind of answer, not when his power—and his daughter—were at stake. Yet he seemed to go along without any argument.

"Thank you, Chief. Mr. Slocum, I'd like a word with you outside." Keller rose, huffed and puffed out, and stopped in the hallway outside the police chief's office.

"You're not getting much for your money," Slocum said. He started to ask why Keller paid off the police in the first place, but the man cut him off with a motion of his hand.

"I want you to take on this task. You are a capable man, and you know more about what is happening than any of those buffoons," Keller said, jerking his thumb in the direction of the chief's office. "Will you do it?"

"I need help. That's why I came to you."

"Here, take this," Keller said, forcing a thick roll of greenbacks into Slocum's hand. "Use the money to buy the information. Don't let Beatrice remain in their obscene yellow hands one instant longer than necessary."

"If Considine comes back, let me know," Slocum said. He doubted a man as shrewd as William Considine would ever return to his employer once it became obvious he was suspected in a kidnapping.

"How do I get in touch with you?" asked Keller.

"I'll be around," was all Slocum said, trying to restrain his anger at the man's attitude. Wealth could be used as a powerful lever to move men and institutions. Keller had shown little inclination to do so to get back his daughter. If anything, his anger at Considine for cheating him at the racetrack overwhelmed every other concern.

It was time for Slocum to stop being so polite.

"A hunnerd dollars is a powerful lot of money," the sewer rat of a proprietor said. His beady eyes darted about, as if worried someone might see him talking to Slocum. "Two hunnerd is even better."

The shooting gallery was deserted at this time of day. Slocum turned, drew his six-shooter in a smooth, quick motion, and fanned off five fast shots. Each hit a target at the far end of the gallery. He turned, his six-gun smoking. Both knew one round remained.

"A hundred dollars in a live man's hand is worth a lot more than two hundred in a dead man's," he said.

"Considine, yeah, I know him. Comes in to shoot a few rows of clay pipes once or twice a week. Seen him last night. Might be back tonight."

"Here," Slocum said, passing over the hundred dollars. It vanished like a rabbit in a stage magician's act. "You send somebody for me when he returns. I'm at the hotel up at California and Bush."

"I know the one. Good place. You got a lot of money."

"Yeah," Slocum said, carefully lowering the hammer and replacing his six-shooter in his holster. "I have a lot of money for the right person, and nothing but death for the wrong one." He left the gallery, found a dingy alley, and hastily reloaded.

He had only seconds to spare when the owner of the shooting gallery popped out and rushed down the street. Slocum knew a hundred dollar bribe would not loosen the man's lips, but it would put grease under his feet. He would run straight for William Considine.

Through the Barbary Coast and North Beach Slocum followed the ratlike man. His quarry headed north to the docks along the bay, then went west toward Fort Point. He stopped before reaching the war-era base. Pacing nervously, he obviously waited for someone. Slocum settled down next to a knee-high wall covered in fragrant, purple bougainvillea and waited.

William Considine showed up less than ten minutes later.

Slocum watched as the shooting gallery proprietor waved his arms around and told Considine about Slocum's visit. Slocum doubted anything was said about the money changing hands. When the man pointed in the direction of the hotel Slocum had claimed to be staying at, he knew he had been sold out. Fear of William Considine outweighed greed and more money from John Slocum.

Considine shoved the man away, then headed in the direction of Bush and California, a mile or so uphill from Considine's Chinatown haunts. Slocum checked his six-gun again, made sure it was ready for action, then lit out after Considine.

It took only a few minutes before Considine grew suspicious and turned to look behind him. He saw Slocum.

"Wondered when you would catch on."

"Did that scum-sucking pig sell me out?" demanded Considine.

"Doesn't matter. Where are Beatrice and Ah So?"

Considine laughed nastily. "Where you'll never find them." He muttered something more to himself that Slocum didn't catch. Then, "You're gettin' to be a royal pain in the ass, Slocum. I thought I took care of you sending you off on a vacation to China."

"Didn't like the accommodations," Slocum said. "Enough of this. I want Beatrice back."

"You and the little spoiled rich bitch? That's funny,

Slocum. She wouldn't give me the time of day. She certainly isn't worth spilling your blood over.''

"I want the Chinese girl, too. And the pearl."

Considine frowned. "Pearl? What pearl?" Then the confusion vanished and he laughed again. "I understand now. How poetic of you. Too bad it won't matter to the sharks. I'm going to kill you and throw you in the bay. This time the sharks will feed on your bloody carcass!''

Slocum saw Considine moving to pull away his jacket, to free the six-shooter holstered under his left arm. Slocum's hand was already in motion. He cleared leather and fanned off two quick shots. One struck Considine in the belly, doubling him up.

Such a wound suited Slocum just fine. He didn't want Considine dying until he told everything he knew. Killing him outright would only send the information he carried to the grave with him.

Considine got off a shot that ripped past Slocum's head, cutting a hole in the brim of his hat. In spite of himself, Slocum jerked. His next shot missed Considine by a country mile.

Then he wasn't sure what happened.

A heavy wagon lumbered along, the driver oblivious to the gunfire around him. The draft horses blocked Slocum view for a moment. He ducked low, trying to get another shot at Considine between the wheels of the wagon. All he saw was dust kicked up by the iron-clad wheels.

Yelling, Slocum jumped to the far side of the street to get another shot at Considine.

The man had vanished into thin air.

12

Slocum had never worked harder as a tracker. Pedestrians and riders passing by stared at him curiously as he dropped flat on his belly and studied the ground for blood. He had winged Considine. He saw the bullet hit the man in the belly and double Considine over. But Slocum had never seen him go down. That worried him.

. Too often, Slocum had seen a bullet hit a man's huge belt buckle or something hidden away in a pocket. He remembered the armory Considine carried with him. Knives, derringer, six-shooter slung in the underarm shoulder, who knows what else he might have tucked about his body like some cardsharp gambler?

Slocum slithered along in his hunt for spoor. Too many people had passed this way for the ground to be smooth before Considine had tromped on it. And Slocum could not find even a single drop of blood. Even if he had winged Considine, the man might have held in the blood long enough to get away.

A half hour of hunting turned up nothing. Slocum wished he had some idea where Considine had been prior to meeting the rat-faced shooting gallery proprietor. The tall, bulky man had to be holed up nearby, otherwise he couldn't have disappeared so quickly and easily.

Slocum hated to admit it, but he had lost William Considine. His only chance at finding Beatrice and Ah So had vanished in the span of a few frenzied heartbeats.

Slocum set off to get his horse. He had some riding to do. Again.

The snooty butler let Slocum into Keller's house right away, but he still looked down his Roman nose at Slocum, as if he had just come in from the stables without cleaning his boots. When the butler knocked discreetly at the solid oak door, the magnate bustled out from his study, his jowls bouncing and his face redder than a beet.

"Did you find that blackguard?" Keller demanded without preamble.

"I winged him, but he got away," Slocum said. Keller's expression betrayed very little. He might have been glad at this report, but what sparked the hint of joy that came and went faster than lightning? That Considine was hit or that he got away scot-free?

"I have asked various . . . associates about Considine and Little Pete. They have nothing constructive to add to what we already know." Keller spoke with finality, but Slocum knew it was only beginning. Beatrice was still in the clutches of—who?

"Has anyone sent a ransom demand for your daughter?" Slocum asked.

"No, no one has asked for 'ary a red cent," Keller said, startled at the question. Slocum remembered Beatrice's insistence that her father would not pay a ransom for her. Had he received a demand or not? Slocum did not know.

"After I shot Considine," Slocum said, emphasizing that Keller's assistant was walking around with a bullet in his gut, "I tried to find anyone who might know where your daughter is. No one will fess up to knowing anything."

"Not surprising, Mr. Slocum. This city is divided into parts where even I cannot venture, where my name and money have no effect."

Slocum did not believe that any more than he did that Chief Gordon was unable to find so much a tiny thread to follow back to a more productive ball of information. Keller played a game different from Slocum's, and it hardly mattered if Beatrice was rescued safe and sound.

"There is one source I have not tried," Keller said, for the first time reflecting his uncertainty.

"How do we get there?"

"Mr. Slocum, this is most dangerous. I am not sure I want to try, but my daughter's safety is at stake. You do not have to accompany me."

"I will," Slocum said. And that was how he descended into hell.

The butcher shop smelled of death. Blood ran in sluggish rivers on the floor, and the Chinese butcher took far too much glee in having Henry Keller begging for anything dealing with his daughter.

"Are you sure it is the Bo Sin Seer that has taken her?" asked Keller. He mopped his red face with a linen handkerchief, totally out of place in the midst of severed chicken parts. For all that, Keller did not appear discomfited by the strong coppery blood odors or the dingy, dark surroundings.

The butcher nodded once, then looked at Slocum, studying him. Slocum remained impassive, not wanting to give the man the impression he was as desperate as Henry Keller. Trying to read the butcher's dark eyes proved as hard as deciding what lay in a professional gambler's hand held close to the vest.

"We need to hire men to come with us," Keller said. The response was as emphatic as it was immediate.

"No! None must enter the *ways*. You must sneak in. No police, no vigilantes, no army must enter."

"What are you saying?" Slocum felt the jaws of a trap closing.

"If you come with many, many men, they will hide. They are clever, they know the underground ways too well. The tong hatchet men are like the moles under your feet, burrowing all the time, coming up only at night and to bite. You must only go alone." The butcher wiped his hands on a filthy rag and stared at Keller.

"He doesn't go anywhere without me," Slocum said.

The butcher gave his slight shrug again. Slocum wasn't sure what that meant, but he intended to accompany Henry Keller in his hunt. And he wanted the magnate to pay after they had found Beatrice.

"Now," the Chinese butcher said. "Pay now." He held out a bloodstained hand and wiggled the fingers in what Slocum could only think of as a man demanding graft. "Otherwise, no show you any of the *ways*."

Slocum had his six-shooter out, cocked, and aimed at the man's face before he could reach for the cleaver stuck in the wood cutting block.

"Money after we find Mr. Keller's daughter."

"Information is expensive. I risk my life even speaking with you," the butcher said.

"Half now, half later," Keller said, getting into the spirit of the dickering.

"All," insisted the Chinese butcher. Slocum saw how adamant the man was on this point. He might not like it, but they went nowhere without the man's information. How Keller had come upon this hacker of animal parts Slocum was at a loss to say, but he seemed to know what they needed. He had described both Beatrice and Ah So fairly well, then mentioned the tongs and their battle. This might be common knowledge throughout Chinatown, but the butcher was the first—and only—resident along Dupont Gai to agree to even speak with them.

The deciding bit of information had come when the butcher claimed William Considine was down in the underground maze of tunnels. This fired up Keller to the point where there was no holding him back.

Henry Keller grumbled and fumbled as he pulled out a zippered wallet. He counted out the bills one by one, as if each cost him another bit of his soul. For all Slocum knew, that might be true. He still had little notion how Henry Keller made his money.

"Good, good," the butcher said, making the greenbacks disappear as if by magic. "Come this way." He scuttled toward the rear door and led them into an alley. To the left ran the bustle of Dupont Street. In the other direction lay a tangle of buildings, each blocking the alley more effectively than the one in front of it. The firetrap they went to in that direction needed only a single spark to send it up in flames.

"Here?" asked Slocum. He rested his hand on the butt of his six-gun.

"Not here. Down. Inside we will find the entrance to the underground ways."

"What are they?" asked Keller, mopping his forehead again with his handkerchief. He gasped and panted as if he had run the entire way. Slocum wasn't sure the millionaire would be able to keep up if the going got rough.

"They lead to opium dens," the butcher said in a conspiratorial whisper. "Slavers use them to move their human wares from one spot in Chinatown to another. There are other, more evil reasons for walking under the streets in the cramped tunnels."

"I've heard of them," Keller said, looking apprehensive. "They go for miles."

"And deep," the butcher assured him. "Many, many feet deep under the streets. The opium smokers do not like to be disturbed when they begin their happy sleep."

"No one's going to be happy if we don't find Miss Keller." Slocum glared at the butcher to let him know what he might expect if he tried double-crossing them. The man's face turned impassive, and Slocum read noth-

ing there. He still suspected treachery. Everyone had
worked to lie to him and cheat him since he had lost his
money at the racetrack.

The butcher crowded through a narrow door and vanished into the building. Slocum and Keller followed more
cautiously. Slocum strained to hear anything that might
alert to him a trap. The building settled and moaned as if
a thing alive, but he heard nothing more than the scurry
of rats. The shuffling sounds of the butcher's slipper-clad
feet stopped ahead.

"Are you armed?" Slocum asked Henry Keller. It had
not occurred to him to remind Keller to bring a weapon.
Slocum hoped he knew enough to do it on his own. Somehow, he did not feel too reassured when Keller patted a
side pocket.

The bulge was hardly large enough for a six-shooter.

"Here, quickly. In. You must hurry down before they
see you!"

"The tongs?" asked Slocum.

"Yes," came the sibilant hiss. A hand pushed into the
small of Slocum's back. "Down the steps, chop-chop.
Follow the corridor until you find what you seek."

"Wait, I want to be certain—" Henry Keller cut off
his sentence when it became apparent the butcher had left,
fading into the shadows in the tumbledown building and
vanishing like a ghost.

"What do you think, Slocum?"

"I think we're damned fools for going down there,"
Slocum said, staring into the darkness. Faint sweet odors
wafted up, hinting at the illicit opium dens hidden away.
"I'll go first."

It had been dark in the warehouse. Slocum slipped beneath the waves of gloom and almost drowned in the
murky underground. His broad shoulders brushed rough
planking that gave way as he walked forward slowly. Un-
derfoot was only a sticky softness; Slocum had no idea
what lay beneath his boot soles, and he did not want to

know. Behind, he heard the grunting and puffing of Henry Keller as the man tried to fit himself into the narrow passageway.

"What's ahead, Slocum? I can't see a thing."

"Opium den," Slocum whispered. He pushed against a panel and revealed double rows of bunk beds. Near a table with an alcohol lamp and a blue-burning flame sat a man who looked to be a hundred years old.

Wizened hands shook as he rolled a black bead of the waxy raw opium onto a needle. He held the needle in the flame and roasted it. Only when it had achieved a smoky, nutty aroma did he transfer the bead to a pipe with a narrow bowl and a long, thin stem. The old Celestial spent several seconds working to light the bead in the pipe, then lay back on a pallet in the lower bunk and puffed contentedly.

"Damned hopheads," grumbled Keller. "We will never get any information from them."

"These aren't the ones we want," Slocum said. Somehow, the idea of Little Pete or any of the Gi Sin Seer smoking opium until they were insensate seemed unlikely. He guessed the same held true for the Bo Sin Seer. They were criminals who ran opium dens, not the addicts who lay stretched out on the beds in a stupor.

"Who runs this place? They might know what we want."

"Fair question," Slocum allowed. He slipped into the opium den and walked the length, hunting for anyone who might be collecting the money. He frowned at the far end. No one obviously ran the place. Either the entrance was hidden or he had missed something important.

He bent over and grabbed a thin wrist. The taut parchment skin throbbed with a vitality belying the owner's condition. On impulse, Slocum jerked hard and pulled the skeleton of a man from the bunk. Dark eyes shot open, hot eyes unveiled with the smoke of opium.

"You in charge?" Slocum asked.

He dodged back in time to avoid the knife that sought his belly. Slocum punched hard, but the wily Oriental was already moving, ducking out of range. The Celestial pressed against a wall panel and simply vanished.

"Through the wall. The entire place is a honeycomb," Slocum shouted to Keller. He kicked hard and battered down the wall, sending splinters flying everywhere. Slocum didn't want to take the time finding the catch. He plowed forward, six-shooter leveled and hunting for a target. Behind him, he heard Henry Keller moving more slowly, but coming nonetheless.

"Slocum, wait! I can't keep up!" the millionaire gasped.

Slocum did not wait. He rushed forward—and crashed into another thin wooden panel. He rebounded, then turned and kicked like a mule. The wall exploded into a thousand pieces, but Slocum had scant opportunity to appreciate his skill. A hatchet tumbled dimly through space and crashed into the wall beside his head.

Ducking and firing at the same time, Slocum thought he might have hit the hatchet man, but he could not be certain. He fired again, just to keep the killer honest.

His bullet ripped through empty space.

Then he was almost knocked over by Henry Keller running into him from behind.

"What's happened?" wheezed Keller, a small-caliber pistol in his hand. His huge paw dwarfed the gun and made it look more like a toy than anything that might take a man's life—or save Beatrice Keller's.

"Ambush," Slocum said, moving around the tiny alcove. He found the exit and cautiously opened it into another long, narrow corridor. Slocum paused. He had gotten turned around and didn't know where he was.

"Slocum, here. Stairs leading down," panted Keller. The hefty man took out a handkerchief and wiped his forehead. Slocum couldn't tell that it did any good. The instant the cloth left Keller's florid face, more sweat beaded up.

"Do we want to go that way? The stories I've heard say there are dozens of levels. We need to know more. We need a guide to help us find Beatrice in this maze."

Slocum tried to get his bearings, but sounds just behind the walls kept distracting him, almost as if the hatchet men worked to spook him rather than to kill him. He turned to Keller and stopped dead in his tracks. The expression on the man's face was not what Slocum had expected. It was almost . . . triumphant.

Even as the thought crossed his mind, Keller's expression melted back into one of concern and even fear at being trapped so far under Chinatown. He backed off and pointed his pistol down the stairs.

"Are we going down?"

"We won't find Beatrice or Ah So," Slocum said. "Not down there, not anywhere in this tangle of moving walls and doors."

"You're giving up so easily? Considine is here somewhere. I feel it in my bones!"

"We've been snookered," Slocum said. "The butcher might know more than he told us, but we'll never rescue your daughter. I doubt she's even down here."

"Why would the man lie to me? I paid him handsomely!"

Again Slocum had the feeling Keller was hiding something, that his trip into the underground spelled a victory rather than defeat.

"Money won't buy everything," Slocum said. "Most of the Chinese fear the tongs. They won't tell us what we want because you have a lot of money."

"But how will we find Little Pete and get my daughter back?"

Slocum shook his head. He wasn't sure Little Pete had Beatrice, but he wondered at Keller's insistence that the tong boss did.

Slocum found a rickety staircase leading up. He emerged in an alley off Dupont Gai and didn't even bother looking behind to see if Henry Keller had followed.

13

"He stole my money. That yellow monkey robbed me!" raged Henry Keller. The man grew even redder in the face and his dewlaps bobbed over his celluloid collar as he angrily paced back and forth in his study. He rubbed his hands together as if trying to get filth off them.

Slocum watched the millionaire and wondered at his reaction to rooting about under the streets of Chinatown. The entire trip was a wild-goose chase, but Keller had insisted. Moreover, he had insisted on accompanying Slocum in the hunt for William Considine, Little Pete, and the tong hatchet men kidnapping his daughter. Once in the burrows of the opium dens, Slocum wasn't sure if Keller had enjoyed the hunt or if some other, darker emotion had taken over. The idea of finding Considine had excited the man, but the notion he might discover his daughter's kidnappers had not seemed paramount.

Slocum couldn't figure Keller out. He always seemed more worried over losing a dollar than anything else.

Slocum snorted in disgust at this thought and realized he was painting himself with the same brush. He had gotten himself involved in this deadly confusion because Little Pete had drugged horses and cheated him out of eight

114

hundred dollars. He was a good one to talk about thinking of money first and lives second.

Still, the few times Henry Keller mentioned Beatrice, it was hardly as a loving, caring father would. With the resources Keller commanded, including most of the San Francisco police force, he ought to have an army of men making a door-to-door search of Chinatown. It would flush out Little Pete and his fellow tong members from hiding and might even locate Beatrice.

"Have you asked around to see if any of your staff has seen Considine lately? He might have returned for some of his belongings."

"No one's seen him," Keller said, dismissing the notion as absurd with the wave of a pudgy hand. "They would tell me. I wouldn't have to interrogate them."

"You know your hired help better than I do," Slocum said, staring past Keller into the hallway where the butler stood with arms crossed over his chest. Charles listened to every word said in the study, even as he tried to seem unconcerned about it. Where would Charles repeat all he heard? Into William Considine's ear?

"I have made certain inquiries that might bear fruit. I am not sure if they will pay off quickly enough to be of any use. We must hurry. I feel the pressure of time."

"With no ransom demand, that is worrisome," Slocum said, carefully choosing his words. The more Keller rambled on, the warier Slocum became. "I doubt we'd get anything from any of the Celestials even if we killed a chance of them."

"They are nothing but sojourners, here only to take our money and then return to their awful home," Keller said. "How can you trust a man like that?"

"A man working long hours for pitiful wages to make a living and to support a family in a poor country?" Slocum knew his sarcasm fell on deaf ears. Keller ranted on. Slocum leaned back in the soft chair and closed his eyes, thinking hard. One thing Keller said struck a true chord.

Time was running out. With no ransom demand, it was well nigh impossible to figure out who had kidnapped Beatrice and Ah So.

One of the tongs had been responsible for taking the women, but Little Pete would lord it over Keller and try to extort as much money as possible if the Gi Sin Seer had any part in the kidnapping. It would be a mark of distinction for the crime boss. Slocum smiled wryly. He didn't know the Chinese gang lord well, but he reckoned Little Pete would ask for Heavy Seas in return for Beatrice Keller. That would appeal to Little Pete's twisted sense of justice.

But the other tong, the Bo Sin Seer, might as easily have taken both Ah So and Beatrice. Or had one tong taken one and the other spirited off the remaining woman? They might be arguing between themselves for possession of Ah So, using Beatrice Keller as a pawn.

"The emperor's pearl," Slocum said quietly.

"Eh, how's that?" Keller's full attention turned to Slocum.

"Something Ah So said before the highbinders captured her. She might be the linchpin for everything. I think she robbed the Chinese emperor of a very precious pearl."

"A pearl? Worth how much?" Keller canted his head to one side, as if trying to imagine the size of the unknown bauble.

"Not worth your daughter's life," Slocum said, heaving himself to his feet. "Keep on the lookout for Considine or Little Pete. I think finding one of them will unearth the other from under the same damp rock. Let me know if you find them."

"Considine," Keller snarled, his fists tightening. "He cannot get away with double-crossing me like he did."

"I've got to go," Slocum said, not wanting to spend any more time with Henry Keller than necessary.

"Wait, Mr. Slocum. Where will you be?"

Slocum hesitated. He had no reason not to tell Henry Keller of his plans. "Around," was all he said as he left.

Henry Keller had not given him the lead he required. The San Francisco police either wouldn't or couldn't find Beatrice and Ah So. Slocum knew better than to think he could catch one of the highbinders and force him to speak. Even if he found one willing to talk, he wouldn't necessarily understand the man's language—no matter that the Chinaman understood him.

Slocum knew the way to unravel everything lay in William Considine, but he was as slippery as an eel to find and catch. That left two people who might give Slocum a way to track down Keller's former assistant. Captain Jed, the shanghaier, was one, but Slocum doubted he could find him without causing bigger waves than he could swim through. That left the madam in the brothel where Considine had met the shanghaier. But first, Slocum had a small chore to tend to.

He rode straight into San Francisco and slowly around Portsmouth Square. As he reached the far side of the large area, he saw Keller's butler across the crowded open area. Whether the millionaire had sent Charles, or William Considine did, to keep track of Slocum might be of interest. The butler could give Slocum the information he needed, should it be Considine who employed him.

"For another day," he decided. He didn't want to burn that bridge for a while yet, should Keller have sent his servant out rather than Considine.

Slocum rode deliberately to lull Charles into a false sense of security. Then he put his heels to the piebald horse's flanks and galloped down a short alley. Slocum whipped the reins back and forth to keep the horse running until he reached Market Street, then jerked to a halt and jumped off the horse, walking the panting animal in and out of the clanging trolley cars and lumbering wagons. This let him vanish in the crush of traffic and let him work his way south toward Mission Dolores. The old Spanish church provided Slocum another quick path to the west through the cemetery, and then he mounted again and rode at a more leisurely pace until he reached the ocean.

The Pacific was leaden and storms threatened. That mirrored the way Slocum felt. He had been run around too much, had seen a side of San Francisco he cared to leave alone. It was time to fetch Beatrice Keller and be done with the tongs.

He rode to the top of the Twin Peaks and looked down over the city. A fog hung like a suffocating brown saddle blanket, stifling the buildings. But he was less interested in the city than he was in the paths leading to the peaks. The only people moving along the trails lived on the slopes. Unless Charles was a remarkable tracker, Slocum had lost the butler with his quick riding and sharp maneuvering.

Only then did Slocum head for the brothel in the Barbary Coast to ask the madam some pointed questions.

He rode down into the layer of brown smoke and coughed a little, but he never slackened his pace across town. It took him until almost sundown to reach the whorehouse. Slocum cursed this bad luck since drunken sailors now frolicked along the streets, hunting for feminine companionship in a city where there were two hundred men for every woman.

Slocum snorted. There were ten thousand men for every proper woman.

He rode around to the rear of the brothel and tethered his horse. He checked his six-shooter and only then circled to come up to the front porch. Women laughed shrilly at coarse jokes. Slocum paused a moment, remembering the times he had been in such places. He had not behaved much differently, for all his Southern upbringing.

He went to a window and peered in. A sailor sprawled

back on the couch in the sitting room, a skinny redhead rifling through his pockets to steal the few dollars he had left after hitting most of the saloons along the Embarcadero. Two women tended another sailor, plying him with drinks that had no doubt been doctored. They forced him to drink, but refused to share.

The trim, dishwater blonde madam caught his attention. She talked with a brawny man with more muscle than brain. Slocum had seen more than one bouncer in his day. This was no customer but an employee of the brothel. When the madam finished talking to him, he went and stood beside the door, hands hanging loosely at his sides. The huge quart-jar sized fists that formed when someone knocked on the door alerted Slocum to the futility of fighting this man.

Slocum kept moving, finding another window. He wiped a clean spot on the pane in time to see the madam climbing the stairs to the cribs. He stepped back and saw the overhang. Gathering his feet under him, he jumped and caught the edge of the roof and swung up to lie flat on the shingles. Wiggling forward, Slocum got to a window and peered in.

A whore and her customer were on the bed. From the sounds coming from the room, the man was enjoying the session more than the woman, who sounded and looked bored. Slocum rolled to the side and stuck his head into an empty room. Not hearing anyone approaching in the hallway outside, Slocum dropped into the room and went to the door. Opening it slightly, he saw a small antechamber from which opened a half dozen rooms with the stairs leading down opposite Slocum.

He knew what went on in the room next to this one. He quickly moved into the antechamber and checked for light coming under the doors. He went to one a couple paces away and gently tested the doorknob. The knob turned.

Slocum opened the door carefully and peeked inside.

A slow smile crossed his lips. He spun into the room and closed the door behind him.

The madam looked up from her rolltop desk, startled at the intrusion. When she realized the danger facing her, she reached for a cubbyhole. Slocum moved faster and caught her wrist.

"No," he said, twisting the derringer from her grip. "Not until after we talk can you play with your toys."

"I'd rather play with you," she said, batting her long eyelashes at him. She had switched tactics easily and smoothly, seeing she wasn't going to get a chance to gun him down.

"I want to talk to you. Nothing else," Slocum said. He tossed the small pistol onto the bed.

"Not many just want to talk, not when you can have all this—and more." She turned in the desk chair and ran her hands down her sides, pulling the satin dress tighter around her thin frame to emphasize her apple-sized breasts and narrow waist. Tossing her head, a wave of the dirty blonde hair fluttered back from her face. She licked her lips in what she thought was a sexy move.

It wasn't that Slocum was immune to her charms. In his day he had desired women who looked and acted far worse than the blonde madam. He simply remembered Beatrice Keller and how much more she had to offer a man.

"I want something more than to talk," Slocum said.

"I knew it! We can—"

"I want information about Ah So."

"What?" The woman blinked, her brown eyes confused at this sudden turn. "I don't know what you're talking about." She moved to the edge of the chair, ready to bolt—or scream. Slocum drew his six-shooter and laid it on the table where she could see it. A flash of fear on the woman's face convinced Slocum she wasn't going to call out for the bouncer downstairs.

"A Chinese girl."

"We don't trade in them," she said arrogantly. "If you want a Chinee bitch, you get your ass on down to Chinatown."

"Ah So has been kidnapped by a tong. She knows about the emperor's pearl," Slocum said. He saw the greed light up the woman's thin face.

"Pearls? Is there some way *we* can get these pearls? Anything owned by the Chinese emperor must be worth a fortune."

"Might be, but it's the girl I'm hunting for."

"I don't have any contact with the tongs. For all that, I don't allow anyone from Chinatown into this house."

"Just shanghaiers like Captain Jed," Slocum said.

"So? He's a good man, free with his money and he can hold his liquor. The girls like him. He's a gentleman."

Slocum started to argue and backed off. He wasn't here to track down the shanghaier. He wanted Beatrice Keller and Ah So.

"Maybe William Considine knows where Ah So is being held," Slocum suggested. Mention of Considine caused the woman's eyes to widen slightly, then she turned sly.

"Billy is a special customer," she said. "But I don't know much about his business."

"I think he owns this house," Slocum said. The expression on the woman's face proved unreadable. Slocum had taken a shot in the dark about the real proprietor of this bawdy house and seemed to have missed. He quickly changed his tack and asked, "Who does own this place?"

"I run it," she said warily.

"You don't keep the bulk of the money," Slocum said, grabbing the ledger book open in front of her on the desk. Neat rows of numbers showed how much money flowed in and the large portion that was paid out. "Who gets this?" He tapped the ledger.

"If you find out, you're a dead man," she said in a

choked voice. "Don't make me tell, or he'll kill me for sure."

"Considine?"

"Look, mister, I don't know nothing about any pearls or a Chinee whore. Making me tell you about the business isn't going to get any of those things for you. It's only going to get you dead."

"I want to find another woman who's been kidnapped. Beatrice Keller." As he spoke, the madam turned white. Her trembling hand went to her lips.

"You know where she is? If you do, tell me. Her father can make it worth your while." Slocum reached into his pocket and pulled out a few of the greenbacks there. The woman's eyes darted from the scrip to Slocum's green eyes and back to the money.

"I want more, a lot more. I can tell you enough to make it worth your while." She shook her head as if arguing with herself, then added, "I don't know where the girl is, but I can put you onto someone who can help."

"I'm sure you can get a lot more from Henry Keller," Slocum said. Again, the woman jumped as if he had stuck her with a needle. "What can you tell me?"

"Down at the Cobweb Palace out at the north end of Meiggs's Pier, there's a barkeep who knows everything that goes on. His name's Clancy. I've heard tell the women are being sold as whores, but I don't know where. We would never keep any girl against her will here."

"Thanks," Slocum said, a cold knot in his belly. The thought of Beatrice being sold to any derelict with a quarter in his pocket sickened him. He paused and asked, "Who *does* own this place?"

A sour look crossed the woman's face. She opened her mouth to speak but only blood gushed out. Slocum staggered back from her and only vaguely realized he had heard glass breaking and the report of a six-shooter. The window behind the woman was shattered. Slocum rushed to it, Colt in hand.

The fog had moved in, but he caught sight of a large, dark-cloaked form slipping away in the street. Slocum raised his six-shooter and fired three times, but the bullets were swallowed by the fog, and he had no sense he had hit the madam's murderer.

14

Slocum heard heavy pounding on the stairs outside and knew the bouncer was coming to see what the commotion was. With a quick motion, Slocum scooped up the money intended to bribe the madam; she wasn't going to need it. Using the butt of his pistol, Slocum knocked out the shards of broken glass and jumped onto the porch roof. He rolled to the edge and swung down, landing hard on the weedy lawn. Without slowing, he hurried to his horse and mounted.

The piebald shied, and Slocum fought a moment to get the horse under control. Then he set off into the softly enveloping fog to find the man who had shot the madam in the back of the head.

He hadn't ridden a hundred yards when he realized this was a fool's errand. The cloaking fog pulled in tight around him and prevented both sight and sound. The mist swallowed whole the noises he needed for good tracking, and the damp grayness might as well have been a blindfold pulled around his eyes. In resignation, he gave up the hunt for the killer.

"Considine?" he wondered aloud. Whoever had shot the woman had been one hell of a shot. From the street, with fingers of obscuring fog drifting around, it had been the work of a marksman. All the highbinders he had seen preferred small-caliber pistols or their abominable hatchets and knives. Somehow, though he had not gotten that good a look at the murderer, Slocum thought the man had been white.

In the direction of the whorehouse came loud, angry cries. He guessed everyone inside now knew their boss was dead. The actual owner of the brothel might be out more than a few dollars, Slocum mused. With the madam gone, no one remaining would know who the actual owner was. If the man financing the den of prostitution had any brains, he would simply write off the entire operation and never try to collect on the house or the land under it.

"Considine," he said again, considering the woman's reaction when he had mentioned William Considine. She might have been trying to divert Slocum and make him think someone else was responsible for running the house, the shanghaiing, and all the rest of the illicit activity done there.

Had she really known anything of the kidnapping? She had reacted powerfully when Slocum finally mentioned Beatrice Keller's name. The madam had not known Ah So and had been intrigued only when valuable pearls were mentioned.

Head hurting from trying to piece it all together, Slocum rode through the fog, passing within feet of men before even noticing them. He had the uneasy feeling of being watched, but he knew that was unlikely. The hooker's murderer could no more see him than he could anyone else in this pea soup fog.

Now and again, Slocum stood in the stirrups to get a better look at street signs in the flickering light from gas lamps irregularly spaced along the cobblestone streets. He worked his way toward the docks to find the Cobweb Palace the woman had mentioned. He put his horse into a stable a few blocks away, then walked back, taking in the action around him.

More than one shooting gallery provided great amusement for the seamen and others who frequented the dockside dives. Gangs of roving specials patrolled the area, more to keep their hands in the tills of the businesses than to prevent crime. Slocum avoided the policemen and the gangs of hoodlums preying on the drunks.

Inside the Cobweb Palace he quickly learned how it got its name. He ducked as a cursing parrot dived low and took a patch from his hat before soaring to the rafters, cleverly flying through the dangling cobwebs. A single match would set the entire place ablaze.

Slocum wondered at how the saloon had avoided such a fate because of the rowdies inside. The ones who weren't drunk were working hard to get that way, and the barkeep with big walrus moustaches did everything in his power to get them inebriated, even pouring two drinks at the same time in a dexterous move the like of which Slocum had never seen.

"What's your poison? We got a fine French brandy," the barkeep said when Slocum bellied up to the bar. "Or champagne. A bottle of it will attract the finer among our ladies." The barkeep twirled his mustaches and pointed to a table filled with soiled doves.

Slocum didn't have a taste for brandy mixed with nitric acid or the kind of poison he'd likely find with any of the women. He pulled out some of the greenbacks and spread them on the counter.

"I've got special tastes. If you're Clancy, I heard tell you might help fill them."

The barkeep's thick-fingered hand pressed the bills flat. Slocum kept him from spiriting them away before he got his information.

"How special?" the bartender asked. "We can do— dammit!" The barkeep ducked as the parrot swooped down and nipped at him. The entire flight was punctuated with curses in several languages, a couple of which Slocum could not identify. "The damned feathered monster! I wish I'd never set eyes on him. A sailor traded it for a bottle. Cusses in nine languages I can recognize."

The parrot flapped hard to avoid groping hands and then perched back on a cobwebby rafter, watching for another opportunity to wing down in pursuit of more food and torment.

"You can buy a shotgun and finish off the bird," Slocum said. He tapped his fingers atop the barkeep's hand. "I want a Chinese girl. A special one."

"Well, that's a mite hard to do," the barkeep said. "They keep to themselves. Don't know of a single house catering to white men."

"You're not being too helpful," Slocum said. The barkeep looked around and bent forward.

"Heard tell there's some new talent over on Chestnut, not far from Columbus. Two houses, side by side, one for Celestials and the other for anyone interested in passing a few hours pleasantly. You might sneak from one to the other, if the right people are encouraged proper-like." The barkeep pulled the bills back. Slocum let the money disappear into the man's apron pocket.

"New talent there?"

"A fine little Chinese girl, they say. And in the other place, something really special, maybe more to your liking. From the description, it's not often anything this fine is offered in San Francisco."

"Blonde?" Slocum's heart almost exploded. He had hoped the madam had been wrong about the tong putting Beatrice to work in a brothel. It reinforced his notion that Ah So was more important to the Chinese gangs than Henry Keller's daughter.

The barkeep grinned from ear to ear. "You are going to *really* like this place," he said. He bent forward and whispered the address. "If they haven't worn you to a frazzle, come on back and tell me how it was. I heard some stories, but I want to know from somebody first-hand.''

Slocum nodded and left, letting the barkeep draw his own conclusions as to Slocum's intent. After retrieving his horse, Slocum rode to the address in the shadow of Telegraph Hill. Two houses, lights on in most windows, stood side by side. Into one flowed a steady stream of Chinamen. The other catered only to whites. It didn't take Slocum long to realize he would never get into the Chinese whorehouse without attracting unwanted attention.

Besides, Beatrice Keller might be in the other bawdy house, held against her will and sold to the highest bidder. He had sought Ah So because he thought it might be easier to find people willing to talk about a Chinese girl rather than a financial powerhouse's offspring.

He walked to the front door and rapped confidently. The door opened a few inches as the manservant eyed him.

''Come on in, sir,'' the man finally said. He opened the door and permitted Slocum to enter a parlor. Three girls, dressed only in frilly undergarments, lounged there, legs hiked over the arms of couches in what they thought was a provocative display. Slocum had eyes for none of them. Beatrice wasn't there.

''How can I help you?'' asked the madam, a tall, well-built brunette. She licked her lips and took a second look. ''Come to think of it, how can you help *me*?''

''Aw, Rita, you're always hoggin' the good lookin' ones. He's the first guy all night what doesn't look like his cock's gonna fall off from the clap.''

Rita silenced the skinny redhead who had spoken with a cold stare. ''Now, Melinda, don't go talking like that to a customer.''

''I don't mind,'' Slocum said, taking Rita's arm and steering her from the room so he could talk privately. ''Fact is, Clancy told me you had something new and different. Something blonde and green-eyed. I like women with emerald eyes.'' He stared into Rita's muddy brown eyes.

''Melinda there's got green eyes, but—''

''Blonde,'' Slocum said. ''And fresh. I don't mean any disrespect, but that one in the parlor looks rode hard and put away wet.''

Rita laughed. ''She used to work the bagnios over in the Barbary Coast. A dime a poke she charged. I get some use from her when the sea dogs come barkin' at my door.''

''But something healthy?'' Slocum asked.

''Happens I do. Upstairs. But it's not for just anyone.''

Slocum silently passed over what remained of the money he had taken from the shanghaiing captain's lock-box. The madam riffled through the bills and then tucked them into her bodice. She took Slocum's arm and personally escorted him up the stairs.

''We have to keep her under lock and key,'' she said, taking out a skeleton key and opening the door. ''Everyone's after her.''

Slocum pushed the door open and saw Beatrice tied to the bed. She started to cry out in joy when she saw him.

Loudly, he said, ''This looks exactly like what I'm hankering for. Do I keep her tied up so she won't run away?''

''Whatever you want,'' Rita said, winking broadly. ''And if she gets to be too much for you, just call.'' From a side room came a bouncer with a sawed-off shotgun resting in the crook of his arm. With that blunderbuss he could kill everyone in a big room. He would simply turn Slocum and Beatrice to red fog in the small bedroom.

''That won't be necessary,'' Slocum said.

''Karl'll keep watch out here, just so you're not disturbed. Part of the price,'' Rita said. She pushed him gently into the room and closed the door. The key turned in the lock, securing the heavy wood portal.

''John!'' cried Beatrice.

Slocum put his finger to his lips to silence her. He

slowly circled the room and found what he had suspected. A peephole into the next room gave anyone—Rita?—an eyeful of the action in the room.

He sat on the edge of the bed and untied the woman's ankles. As he worked, he spoke in a low voice so only she could hear.

"They're watching. If we do anything they don't like, the bruiser with the shotgun outside will cut us to ribbons."

"Better that than—"

"Quiet," Slocum ordered. He moved over and untied the knots of the ropes around her slender wrists. All Beatrice wore was a thin camisole that did nothing to hide her luscious breasts or the triangle of fleece poking out from between her thighs.

It was crazy, but Slocum found himself responding to her naked beauty in spite of their dilemma. One misstep, and the man with the shotgun would kill them both, and Slocum was all too aware that the peephole was now dark. The madam watched them from the next room.

"Ah So," Beatrice said, scooting closer to him and throwing her arms around his neck. "She's in the house next door. It . . . it is for Celestials only. No white men are allowed in there."

"We have problems besides getting Ah So," Slocum pointed out. He worked his lips close to her ear as he told her of the trap they were in.

"We need to play for time, to think, to lull them into thinking nothing is wrong," Beatrice rattled on.

Slocum knew how they had to act. He kissed her. But he held back. He wasn't used to making love to a woman with an audience all around.

"We *have* to do it, John. There's no other way. They will get bored and tend to other business if they don't see anything amiss in here."

"I hope they don't get too bored," Slocum said wryly. "That'd mean they weren't spying on anything exciting."

"Like this?" Beatrice said, her hand sliding down Slocum's chest and resting on the bulge at his groin. "It's been hell here, John. Men, more men than I can remember. And the only way I stayed sane was to imagine each of them was you."

"I'll just plug the son of a bitch," he started, reaching for his six-shooter. Beatrice stopped him.

"They weren't you. I knew it, and I still longed for you to be with me." She caught his hand and moved it away from his six-gun. Unbuckling his gun belt, she hastily started work on the buttons holding his fly open.

Slocum groaned in pleasure as his erection snapped out, immediately caught by her warm, clutching hand. Beatrice started stroking up and down and Slocum knew having an audience for their lovemaking wouldn't matter to him. He was already lost in the carnal delights Beatrice administered so well.

She moved her hand up and down his length faster and faster until he sank back to the bed. Then she threw one of her long, slender legs over his body, straddling him.

"Come here, cowboy," she said loudly. "Show me how good you can ride." Lowering herself on his steely length made both of them gasp. Beatrice shifted her hips from side to side to get every single inch of his throbbing, hot staff inside her tight passage.

Slocum reached out and brushed aside the silky, thin camisole, taking both her breasts in his hands. Cupping them, he squeezed harder and harder until Beatrice was sobbing with desire. She tossed her head back like a frisky filly and sent a banner of her blonde hair flying. Slocum's fingers found the hard points of her nipples and began tweaking them.

All around his manhood he felt her strong inner muscles squeezing down on him. When she lifted herself up a little in response to his pressure on her mountainous breasts, cool air breezed between their bodies. But only for a moment. She dropped down and totally engulfed him again. Up and down she moved, driving him full-length into her most intimate recesses, but it wasn't enough for Slocum.

His prong trembled and bucked, but it needed more, and he sensed Beatrice wanted more than he was giving. Never had he seen a woman so lovely. He sat up and tried to smother her with kisses. He worked along the line of her jaw, down to her throat and then lower to her breasts until his back threatened to break—or his rigid manhood slip free.

He cupped her buttocks and lifted as he swung his legs around beneath him. They traded places, with Slocum on top now.

"Ride me, cowboy. Show me how you break a bronco," Beatrice gasped out. Slocum wasn't sure if she played to the spying madam and her bodyguard or if Beatrice enjoyed this. From the way she was responding to his every touch, he had to believe she was thrilled with the lovemaking.

He began moving faster and faster, his hips working faster than the pistons on a locomotive. He sank balls deep into her, causing her to lift her legs on either side of his body so he could delve even deeper on the next thrust. When he was sure he would melt from the friction, Beatrice gave a tiny gasp and shivered. She clawed at his back as she gave way to her passionate release.

Then Slocum exploded like a stick of dynamite. Beatrice's legs locked around his waist and held him close until he was completely spent. Only then did she release him and let him drop down atop her. Their bodies were sheened with sweat and both panted hard. Slocum put his lips close to her ear to whisper his message.

"I don't know if they're still watching. I think I hear footsteps. The bouncer might be going away."

"I don't have any clothes, John."

"Does it matter? If you get away, you can get more."

Unexpectedly, Beatrice laughed. "The very idea of

tramping through the streets of San Francisco naked as the day I was born is funny, isn't it?''

"Only if we're both free," Slocum said, reaching for his six-shooter. He had to be sure they were alone, if only for a few minutes. He jumped to his feet and went to the door, dropping to one knee. He rattled the knob gently. It had been locked after him. He peered through the keyhole, trying to see if the bouncer still patrolled the vestibule.

He motioned for Beatrice to put on his shirt to cover her nakedness partially, then stuck his eye back to the keyhole. The small outer room was empty, as far as he could tell. Both the madam and the bodyguard had tired of watching the action, or they might have gone to tend other customers.

"The first thing we have to do is get back to your pa's house and—"

"We don't go anywhere. Not without Ah So," Beatrice said firmly. "I gave her my word I would save her. I will not break it."

Before Slocum could say a word, he heard footsteps on the stairs. There might not be any other way, he knew. They might have to fight their way out.

15

Slocum handed Beatrice Keller the bedspread to pull around her shoulders and hide some of her delightful nudity. In this room it seemed somehow perverse, especially after making love while the madam watched them. Out on the streets, Beatrice's nakedness would draw unwanted attention. Either way, he preferred Beatrice to be covered. His eyes darted to the window in the room, then saw the heavy iron bars blocking the way outside. Getting out of this room would be worse than escaping from the San Francisco jail.

"I *won't* let Ah So go through what I have, John," the partially clad blond insisted, stamping her bare foot angrily. "This is horrible, but I have been able to cope with the, with the—" Beatrice began to sputter and cry as the full impact of everything after the kidnapping came back to torment her.

Slocum shoved her to the bed where she bounced and clutched his shirt around herself.

"Why'd you do that?" she asked, startled.

Slocum didn't have time to explain. He yelled, "Bitch! Shut up or I'll whup you good!" He turned in time to slip behind the door as a key rattled in the lock. The bouncer, Karl, stuck his head in.

"Don't go hurtin' the merchandise, mister," Karl shouted. A blank look on his face when he saw Beatrice alone on the bed was quickly replaced by a feral snarl, but it was too late for him to turn his scattergun around. Slocum brought the barrel of his Colt Navy down as hard as he could on the top of the man's head. Buffaloed, the bouncer crashed to the floor like a felled oak and lay, unmoving.

"Take this," Slocum said, tossing the shotgun to Beatrice. It was a dangerous move because a small mistake on her part would kill more than an intended victim. He worked to get the bouncer out of his pants. He handed them to Beatrice. "See if you can make them stay up. It's better than going out bare-ass naked."

"There is clothing in the other rooms. I've heard Rita talking about it. They sometimes dress up really fancy for special customers."

"No time," Slocum said. The blanket from the bed, his shirt, the bouncer's pants, those would have to suffice until they got Beatrice to safety. He thought a moment, then worked off the bouncer's shoes. He tore pieces of sheet and stuffed them in the shoes so they would fit Beatrice's feet without too much irritation when she walked. He wondered if Little Pete's shoe factory had manufactured them.

"Be damned careful with that shotgun. You can kill everyone in a room with it."

"You take it," she said, pushing it toward him.

Slocum whirled around and fired point-blank into another man's belly. The second bouncer's eyes widened in surprise, then he clutched his stomach and sank to the floor.

"Is there another staircase?" Slocum knew it would be dangerous going to the front parlor. He had no idea what kind of customers Rita entertained there. More than likely, at least one would be willing to fill Slocum and Beatrice full of holes, just for the hell of it.

"There. That door," Beatrice said, her voice weak.

Slocum didn't bother to see if she followed. He gingerly opened the door and found service stairs leading to the rear of the house. He went down the steps two at a time. The kitchen was empty. Beatrice trailed behind, uncertainly clutching the sawed-off shotgun. He took it from her, realizing how risky it had been having her follow him down the stairs. A single slip would have blown his spine to smithereens.

"The tong runs this house and the one next door where Ah So is," Beatrice said.

"The tong? Little Pete's?"

"No, he had nothing to do with the kidnapping. This is all Bo Sin Seer doing."

Slocum snorted in contempt. The only reason Little Pete had nothing to do with Beatrice and Ah So's kidnapping was that the Bo Sin Seer killed all his highbinders and kept him from cashing in on their misfortune. Still, Slocum felt a small glow of pride in his reasoning. He had not thought Little Pete held Beatrice. If the tong leader had, he would have never hesitated to shake every penny possible from Henry Keller.

Slocum opened the rear door leading onto a screened porch, looked around, and then motioned Beatrice to follow. The alleyway behind the brothel led toward Stockton Street. Beatrice followed clumsily, grabbing at her sagging drawers and fighting to keep the blanket around her shoulders.

"No farther, John. We fetch Ah So. I won't budge another inch until you get her."

"We'll both get killed." He saw reason did not sway her.

"She will be killed the instant they learn I have escaped," Beatrice pointed out.

"Maybe not," Slocum said. "Selling you the way they

did tells me they thought they could get more for you whoring than if they ransomed you. Or maybe they didn't even know who you were. You didn't tell them you were Henry Keller's daughter, did you?''

''Why, no.''

Slocum's mind spun. ''They were after Ah So, not you. That must be one passel of pearls she stole for them to go to so much trouble.''

''She is not a thief,'' Beatrice said firmly. ''She is a cultured, sensitive soul. I knew the instant I laid eyes on her she was special. Different, not like the poor peasants making their way through to *Gum San Ta Fow*.''

''What's that?''

''The Golden Gate. San Francisco. John, I insist that we get Ah So. She must not endure another moment as a singing girl.''

Slocum had heard that term used for a whore. He had also heard a lot worse used. Somehow, the idea of Ah So being sold to any Chinaman with a few coins to rub together bothered him as much as finding Beatrice in the house of ill repute. Beatrice had summed it up well. Ah So was not like other peasants shuffling down Dupont Gai in their trousers and never looking up.

''She couldn't be a peasant,'' he said. ''No peasant could have stolen the emperor's pearls.''

''She is *not* a thief, either.''

Slocum pulled Beatrice along until they stood behind the house next door. As quietly as possible, he entered the small rear yard and made his way around the house. If the other had catered to white men, this definitely called to the men from the Flowered Kingdom. The scent of burning joss sticks drifting out an open window made Slocum's nose water. From the side he got a quick look inside. A woman poured tea into a pink and green ceramic bowl and accepted a square of folded rice paper in return.

''He's paying for his soiled dove,'' Beatrice said, her voice cracking with strain. She pressed close to him. Slocum couldn't help noticing the firmness of her breast, the scent of her body, the way her beauty was enhanced by the intensity of her emotion.

"Let's see if we can get in through a cellar window. There's no way we're getting in through any door on this level." Slocum pointed to the highbinders standing with folded arms just inside the entry. He didn't doubt they kept their hands firmly around hidden knives or hatchets.

It took a few minutes jiggling on a cellar window to convince him he wasn't getting in that way. He worked his fingers between the metal frame and the concrete around it and exerted all his strength. Slowly, ever so slowly, the window pulled free of its moorings. It jerked free, and he tumbled back on the ground. The odor of roasting opium gusting out from the cellar made Slocum lightheaded. He squirmed through and dropped to the dirt floor.

"Stay back," he called to Beatrice, but it was too late. She followed, landing in a topsy-turvy heap next to him. Her makeshift clothing was all cockeyed, but she hardly noticed. With as much dignity as she could muster, she stood. Slocum laughed, in spite of the seriousness of their quest.

"We're not alone down here," he said softly. "Listen. I can hear someone breathing."

He went exploring and found a miner's candle on a ledge along the wall. It took several lucifers before he brought forth a pale, flickering yellow light. When he did, he saw rows of wooden bunks like those he and Henry Keller had found under the streets of Chinatown. The difference lay in the occupants. All these contained Chinese women chained at the ankle.

"The sweet smell," Beatrice said, rubbing her nose. "Is that opium?"

"They've drugged these girls," Slocum said, working his way down the line of bunks. He stopped when he came to the last one. Ah So lay sprawled on the narrow pallet, double chains around her ankles and a glazed expression on her face. Her muscles had gone flaccid, a sure sign the opium had worked its frightful enchantment on her.

"Ah So, wake up," cried Beatrice, shaking the Chinese girl. Ah So's eyelids fluttered but she did not awaken.

"She's too far gone. Drugged," Slocum said. On a low table beside the bunk were all the implements of an opium smoker. The long thin roasting needle, a tiny ceramic vessel, a pipe with a long stem and small bowl, and a few beads of the tarry raw opium.

Slocum went to the foot of the bunk. For all the rickety wood in the bunks, the Bo Sin Seer left nothing to chance when it came to chaining their valuable property. The links in the chains binding Ah So's ankles were bright and shiny, brand-new, fastened with a heavy padlock Slocum doubted he could shoot off. He followed the double chains to a thick ring fastened into the wall.

Futile tugs convinced him he would never yank it free. The ring was fastened in the concrete foundation of the house, possibly backed with a large steel plate.

"I need a hacksaw," he said. "See if you can find one. Or any kind of tool."

"What are we going to do, John?"

"Go hunt," Slocum ordered. He saw no way of getting the girl free of the brothel. In her condition, she would have to be carried. But Slocum couldn't even hoist her to his shoulders with the chains securing her.

"I can't find anything. I've looked everywhere. All I found were tins marked 'five taels.' I think they have opium in them."

Slocum went to the waist-high stack of eighteen-ounce tins Beatrice had uncovered. Each held dark fluid the consistency of molasses:opium. Slocum knew there was a fortune in the illicit drug here. Whether the Bo Sin Seer tong used it for their customers upstairs or this was nothing more than a convenient storage area, he neither knew nor cared.

Whichever it was did nothing to help get Ah So free of the tong's clutches.

Slocum looked up the stairs and guessed there would be a locking bar on the far side. The only way out was the way they had entered. Not only were the girls drugged and chained, they had been locked in the cellar to keep them from escaping. Slocum realized how lucky he had been finding a window tractable enough to pry out of its foundations.

"There's nothing we can do for her," he said.

"John, I told you. I will *not* leave until we rescue her."

"She's in no danger right now. I don't think they are using any of these girls upstairs. They are special," he said, studying the slack faces and dazed eyes.

"Why? How?"

Slocum shrugged. He had no answer.

"If we get her out, it'll have to be with an army. I'm not sure I'd get lucky sneaking back in with enough tools to get her free. Even if I did, there's no way I could carry her out alone—or even with your help," he hastily added. To his surprise, Beatrice did not argue.

"What are we going to do? The police?"

Slocum laughed harshly at that. They might go to Beatrice's father, but some gut-level instinct told him to avoid involving Henry Keller. The man played another game, one Slocum wasn't even aware of.

"I have an idea, but you have to be somewhere safe."

"At home?"

"Let's try the old house on Nob Hill," he said, coming to a decision. "Who knows about it?"

"Why, nobody, except perhaps the highbinders. You said they were scouring the area hunting for Ah So."

"The tong," muttered Slocum, "but not Considine or your father?"

"No, not really."

"I'll boost you out of here," he said, the decision coming fast. "And I promise to get Ah So out."

"How?"

"With just the right allies."

After seeing Beatrice safely to the house on Nob Hill, he wasted no time going downhill to Chinatown. The bustle just before dawn was almost as frantic as at high noon. The Chinese never seemed to sleep, always being hard at work in their stores, moving impossibly heavy crates, doing twice the work anyone could expect from another human being.

Slocum knew his presence was noted, and he knew no one would answer any questions he might pose. Slocum had a different notion. He wandered the length and breadth of Chinatown for several hours until he saw two burly Chinese, their long queues bobbing as they walked, collecting the Gi Sin Seer tribute.

Walking boldly up to them as they came from a small curio store, counting their extortion money, Slocum said, "I want to talk to Little Pete."

Both men reached for pistols thrust into silk sashes, then paused when Slocum did not go for his six-shooter. They exchanged glances. Whatever communication passed between them, one hurried off while the other stood stock-still, staring implacably at Slocum.

Saying nothing, Slocum leaned indolently against the building and stared down the street. Within ten minutes, a closed carriage clattered up. The door opened. In the dim interior Slocum saw Little Pete decked out in fancy clothing, as if he intended to go directly to the opera, even though it wasn't even noon.

"Slocum, you think to steal money from me?"

"You stole eight hundred from me," Slocum said in a level tone, "but I am willing to forgive the debt in exchange for a service."

For almost a minute Little Pete did not speak. The Celestial sat in his carriage, staring at Slocum as if taking his measure. Slocum was aware of the two highbinders on either side of him, ready to draw and shoot if their boss ordered it.

"Join me for a ride," Little Pete said. It was not an invitation.

Slocum climbed in. The two highbinders jumped onto steps on the sides of the carriage, where they could keep a sharp eye out as the vehicle rolled along.

"You are a strange man, Slocum. You are given a ride to the Heavenly Kingdom and yet you return to San Francisco. You seek trouble when it does not search for you. Now you tell me I do not owe a debt that I fail to acknowledge."

"Being shanghaied is hardly a free trip. I'll find Captain Jed one of these days and repay him for my brief trip."

"Ah, Captain Jed." From the way he said it, Little Pete might mean anything.

"That's not what I want. There are two brothels over on Chestnut Street run by the Bo Sin Seer."

This caused Little Pete to sit a bit straighter. The tension mounted.

"You know their location?"

"I know one has a pile of opium tins this tall," Slocum said, indicating waist high. "It must be worth a fortune."

"I have little interest in opium. That trade is beneath my contempt."

"You mean there isn't enough profit in it?" Slocum shot back. This caused Little Pete to frown, then the hoodlum laughed.

"A bold move, and one placing you on a knife's edge. If I did not have a good sense of humor, you would be dead for your insolence. My statement stands. The Patna opium smuggled into San Francisco by the Fook Hung Company is of no interest to me."

"The Bo Sin Seer has a lock on the trade, is that the problem? This might give the Gi Sin Seer a chance to move into the other tong's territory."

"The Fook Hung Company is a triad, not a tong," Little Pete said.

The distinction was lost on Slocum, but he saw he was right in his guess. Little Pete was shut out of the opium trade by his rivals.

"A raid on the brothels and seizure of their opium might go a ways toward giving you the upper hand."

"I deal in knowledge, in news no one else admits. If you do not have something important to add to my store of understanding of all facets of life in San Francisco, you waste my time."

"William Considine is behind the opium trade. He has to be the one fronting for the Bo Sin Seer." Slocum spoke with bitterness. "He smuggles it in on Captain Craig's vessel."

Little Pete laughed, gently at first and then with increasing force until tears ran down his sallow cheeks and he held his sides.

"Considine behind the opium trade? No, Slocum, no. Henry Keller is the kingpin responsible for opium smuggling. It is Henry Keller who is responsible for most of the crime in this fine city not controlled by the tongs."

16

"You refuse to help?" Slocum considered his chances of getting out of the carriage if he shot the tong leader in the gut. It wasn't a good bet, he decided. He had knowingly walked into the jaws of a steel-toothed trap.

"No, not at all. I am sure we can come to an accommodation," Little Pete said. "There is other merchandise I deal in besides information."

"For blackmail," Slocum said. Little Pete screwed his face into a smile and nodded. Slocum went on, "Are you blackmailing Henry Keller?"

"Mr. Keller? Ah, no, but for this meddling man I have no affection. He is a most powerful man, but his reach does not extend into Chinatown."

Slocum considered all that had happened. Keller certainly ran the San Francisco Police Department, but why had he agreed to personally go into the tunnels under Chinatown in a vain search for his daughter? There had to be another reason.

"Considine," Slocum said slowly. "Has he double-crossed his boss?"

"You begin to see a glimmering of the truth. No one is totally honorable in these turbulent days. Mr. Considine agreed to aid me in fixing horse races. It so happened one was the race where Heavy Seas lost so badly.''

"So Keller's gunning for his former right-hand man,'' Slocum said. "And Considine is trying to cut in on the opium smuggling, also. That would make Keller angry enough to want to plug him.''

"Ah, you refer to your futile excursion under the streets and into the opium dens. That was a charade for your benefit, I fear. Keller knows there are no real tunnels, only a few set up to impress gullible tourists willing to pay great amounts of money for illicit thrills. It is amazing how many, especially from foreign countries and New York, who believe all they see is real.''

"Why help rescue Ah So?''

"Why would it strain even your faith if I told you I would rescue another citizen of the Heavenly Kingdom from such slavery?'' Little Pete turned and stared out the carriage window. Slocum tried to figure where they went and could not. He didn't know the city well enough. If either of the tong leader's bodyguards decided to stick a knife in him, Slocum doubted there would be anyone around willing to call the police.

Considering that Henry Keller had used him to track down Considine, Slocum knew that, even if the police came, it would do him no good. He only wished he had done a better job. He would have enjoyed gunning down the race-fixing, drug-smuggling, shanghaiing William Considine. The last time he had Considine in his sights, he had not been able to fire the killing round.

"You want to take your war directly to the Bo Sin Seer,'' Slocum said. "But what is their interest in Ah So? They have a cellar full of girls to sell into prostitution.''

"Why do you seek her, Slocum?''

"Beatrice Keller promised the girl she would help. She *is* honorable and keeps her word.''

Little Pete nodded and smiled wryly, as if this had never occurred to him.

"There is a price you must pay for our cooperation. The Gi Sin Seer does not lightly go to war with another tong."

Slocum laughed harshly. From all he had seen, the tongs killed one another—and anyone in the way—at the drop of a hat. But he had expected Little Pete to name a price. He hoped it was something he could pay.

"My bodyguard, Lee Chuck, has been convicted of murdering the police officer. You were there and know it was clearly self-defense."

Slocum knew it was murder, but he held his tongue. Little Pete had a plan to free the burly killer that included John Slocum.

"He soon will be sent to a prison far down the coast. At the time of his transfer, you must rescue him from his captors. If you do this one thing, we will rescue Ah So."

"The police will burn San Francisco to the ground hunting for Lee Chuck. If I get him away, you have to hide him."

"There will be no problem in this respect. He is to be moved this evening. If Lee Chuck goes directly to the docks, a ship will whisk him far away."

"To China?"

"His destination will please all concerned. Lee Chuck will not bother anyone in San Francisco again."

Slocum had no choice, though he knew he was being used as he had been by Henry Keller. This time it was the tong leader tugging him along in directions he cared not to go.

"Two accompany him," Little Pete said. "How you divert them is up to you. Any Chinaman within a hundred yards would alert the guards and bring down dozens more of the blue-coated *kwan fei*. We would avoid such bloodshed."

Slocum listened with half an ear. The police would

bring out Lee Chuck from a door leading directly into the cellblock. The armored wagon would take him to whatever prison had been decreed by the judge. It hardly mattered to Slocum which penitentiary it might be. If he failed, he would follow Lee Chuck into captivity.

"He need only reach the end of the street and turn the corner. From there, Lee Chuck will cease to exist," Little Pete said, pointing down the street. "You must hurry. I hear the sound of keys in locks."

The Celestial turned and backed into a doorway, out of sight of anyone in the street. Slocum started walking, eyes studying the police scattered around the building. Little Pete was right about an army coming down on his head if anything went wrong. It was clever of the tong leader to let a white man do his dirty work, because any Chinese approaching the building would be spotted immediately and stopped.

"Come on out, boys," came a gruff voice. "The way is clear." The turnkey rattled his ring of keys as he opened the steel door and made way for Lee Chuck and his two guards to exit the city jail. The hatchet man walked with his head bowed and his hands chained in front of him. Slocum saw Lee Chuck's legs were also manacled. That would pose a problem.

As a wagon rattled by in the street, Slocum jumped in front and waved his hat. The driver, startled, reined back and started cussing a blue streak. The frightened horse reared and then bolted down the street where the guards worked to load Lee Chuck into their wagon.

"Stop him, stop him!" shouted Slocum. He drew his six-shooter and fired in the air to keep the frightened horse running. The wagon sideswiped the police wagon and sent it skittering, taking one of the guards with it.

For the first time, Lee Chuck looked up. His eyes widened, but he showed no fear. Slocum didn't know if Little Pete had warned him to be alert for an escape, or if the hulking Chinaman simply understood this was his only chance for freedom. He used an elbow on the second guard, sending him reeling.

The turnkey Slocum bowled over. As he scrambled about, Slocum drove his knee into the man's gut. With careful aim, Slocum sighted in on Lee Chuck's ankle chain and fired three more times. One bullet severed a link, freeing the highbinder.

"Stop that wagon. He's a thief!" shouted Slocum. "He robbed me." Another shot at the rapidly disappearing wagon and driver made sure it would never slow down this side of hell.

Slocum canted his head in the other direction, indicating Lee Chuck should run. The Chinaman did—seconds ahead of a flood of blue-suited police pouring from the station to see what the commotion was about.

"That way," panted Slocum, pointing after the fleeing wagon. "He helped the prisoner escape."

Before the fallen guard could gasp out a denial, Slocum bumped into another cop and pushed him on top of the guard on the ground. It would be long minutes before either of them was able to join the fray. Slocum kept his arms swinging and six-gun pointing in the direction opposite to the one taken by Lee Chuck.

"You say they rescued that yellow bastard?" cried a police sergeant.

"That way," Slocum said. He fired his last round and then faded back as more police boiled from the station. They raced after the wagon and its innocent driver, now long gone. Backing away, then turning and walking off as if nothing had happened, Slocum melted into the crowd forming to see what the ruckus was all about.

As he walked along Market Street, he heard a familiar voice behind him call, "Get in, Slocum. We have preparations to make."

"Did Lee Chuck get away all right?" he asked Little Pete.

He wasn't surprised when he received no answer to his question.

"These two houses?" asked Little Pete. The tong leader had transformed from the gaudy peacock decked out in Sunday finery into a shadow barely visible. He wore the more traditional Chinese black alpaca quilted jacket, with an apple-green silk scarf tucked in at the throat. Slocum wasn't sure, but he thought Little Pete clanked as he walked from carrying too many knives and other implements of death hidden about him.

"They're the ones," Slocum acknowledged. "That one is where Ah So is held in the cellar." The other house of ill-repute held nothing of interest for him. From the way Little Pete acted, he shared that opinion.

"The Bo Sin Seer moves far afield. We seldom leave the boundaries of Chinatown for our businesses. It has been good for us to show restraint. They have committed a true error in coming to this spot in the shadow of Telegraph Hill."

Little Pete whistled and assembled more than a score of his men in a circle around him. He spoke in Chinese for a few minutes, then switched to English, possibly to reassure Slocum they worked to achieve the goal he sought.

"We seek the Bo Sin Seer killers. We will wash their bodies."

Slocum knew Little Pete meant they would wash the Bo Sin Seer in their own blood.

"Who has the big dog?" Little Pete nodded as four highbinders held up rifles. "Good. You have the dog food?" Others held up boxes of ammunition. "Puppies?"

Slocum blinked when each of the highbinders pulled a pair of pistols from under their loose fitting jackets. He hadn't seen the like of this firepower since he rode with Quantrill's Raiders. Each man in that bloody-handed band had sported six or eight pistols, giving them the firepower of a band five times their size.

"Let the dogs bark!" cried Little Pete. With this, the highbinders vanished into the night, going to assigned positions. Slocum looked at the tong leader for instructions.

"What now?" he asked.

"They will be in place within minutes. Any coming from the house of singing girls will be shot. When we gauge the response, only then will we attack."

"It'd be better to sneak in and try to rescue Ah So without any gunplay. She might be hurt. You wouldn't want that, would you? You'd never find the emperor's pearls then."

"Pearls?" Little Pete laughed. "Yes, of course, the emperor's *pearls*." He laughed hard, as if Slocum had made a joke. "This is of foremost concern, Slocum."

Before Slocum could push the tong leader to explain the joke, shots rang out. A ragged volley followed, then it sounded as if the war had started anew. Slocum lost track of individual reports. They blended into a roar as if the entire Eleventh Tennessee Regiment had opened fire on the Yankees in Cumberland Gap.

Little Pete drifted like a ghost through the flying lead. Slocum trailed close behind, not sure where the tong boss had positioned his men. Foot-long tongues of orange flame erupted, marking the spots where the snipers fired, but the shorter muzzle flashes from the "puppies"—the six-shooters—came from everywhere.

"They resist more than I anticipated," Little Pete said. "We need to enter quickly or they will kill their hostages."

"Including Ah So?"

Little Pete's dark glare silenced Slocum, as if he said no one would be so foolish. Slocum knew at this instant that Ah So was more important than any pearls she might have pilfered from the Chinese emperor, but he pushed aside thinking too much on that in favor of staying alive.

The air around him sang and buzzed with bullets fired from inside the Bo Sin Seer whorehouse.

"There's too many in there," Slocum said. "They were expecting us."

"That might be so," Little Pete allowed. "We must fight quickly and subdue them before the police arrive. This is not Chinatown. They will not allow a fight to continue forever."

"Get a couple of your men to come with me," Slocum said. "I know where we can get into the basement fast."

Little Pete whistled and four highbinders joined Slocum. He started to give instructions, then decided only to have them follow and keep the Bo Sin Seer from shooting him in the back. Bending low and racing for the rear of the house, he fought past two small knots of tong killers stationed in the alleyway. One of the four with him died of a knife in the throat.

Slocum fired smack into the killer's face to end his murderous days, but he never slowed down to worry about what he was getting himself into. Plunging forward, he reached the side of the house. The three highbinders with him shot at anyone poking a head from the nearby window.

"This is it," Slocum said. He kicked out and dislodged the casement window leading into the cellar. Poking his head through, he glanced around the darkness and could not tell what lay in wait for him.

Slocum took a few seconds to reload his Colt Navy, then squirmed forward again and plunged headfirst into the cellar. He hit, rolled, and fetched up hard against a side wall, six-gun ready for action. The only unusual sounds came from above. The firing became more sporadic as more of the fighters were wounded or died.

Two of the highbinders followed him into the cellar. Slocum took that to mean he had lost another member of his small command.

"This way," he said, working his way down the line

of bunks. The women still sprawled on the thin pallets, eyes glazed from too much opium. When he came to the end of the row, he stopped and looked around in confusion.

"There's supposed to be another bunk here. It's gone." He backtracked and found a vacant bunk. Twin chains dangled, their loops empty.

Ah So was gone.

17

"You lost twelve men?" Slocum was astonished. The fight had been fierce, but he had not realized that much blood had flowed.

"All the others are injured and a few may not survive. That would raise the number killed," Little Pete said, unconcerned. He snapped his fingers and his carriage rattled up. He climbed in, turned in the seat, and waited for a moment, staring at Slocum. The Chinese highbinder gestured for Slocum to join him.

Slocum clambered into the carriage as it rattled off amid the sounds of police whistles and the distant pounding of horses' hooves as the San Francisco Fire Department raced to extinguish the blaze Little Pete's men had started.

"There was no call to burn the house down. A half dozen women were chained to the bunks in the cellar," Slocum said. "They'll all die. Nobody upstairs is likely to save them."

"The Bo Sin Seer intrude in areas where they are not wanted," Little Pete said. "This will be a message to them."

"The message went the other way. They knew we were

coming," Slocum said. "Did someone in your tong leak the information?"

"A traitor? How quaint an idea," Little Pete said, tenting his long yellow fingers and resting his chin on the pinnacle. He was lost in thought as the carriage rattled through the nighttime streets, heading back to Chinatown.

"What do we do about Ah So? She had been moved. That's another reason I think somebody in your organization betrayed you."

"What you say has some merit. However, this city is rife with people collecting and dispensing important facts. After all, that is *my* business."

"I thought you manufactured shoes."

Little Pete frowned in consternation, then laughed. "You continually surprise me with your sense of humor, Slocum. I sell more shoes than anyone else on the Pacific Coast, but no one knows a mere Chinaman owns the American Shoe Factory. All my salesmen are fine, upstanding citizens in their communities. Perhaps a few know they work for a 'yellow monkey,' but if they do find this troubling, their ample paychecks soothe their upset."

"You consider the fight with the other tongs to be your real work? What did the Bo Sin Seer do with Ah So?"

"It is not so much a question of what they did with her but when. Soon, is my guess. They will soon remove her."

"How?"

Little Pete brushed off the question. "She is a perfect flower, or so I am told. It is a shame you fought so well in Oakland. Had we taken her into our custody then, my fighters would have treated her well, unlike those misbegotten jackals of the Bo Sin Seer." Little Pete shrugged his thin shoulders and vented a gusty sigh. "I fear Ah So has sailed beyond my fragile grasp now."

"The other tong has her. Where?"

"She is beyond even your reach, Slocum. Simply desiring something is not the same as getting it. You must learn to live with only that which lies within your reach.''

''I've got a boarding house reach,'' Slocum said. Little Pete did not understand what he meant. The tong leader did not understand that Slocum had the tenacity of a bulldog and the honor of a Southern gentleman. He had promised the Chinese girl he would not permit her to be whisked away—and he had failed. That broken assurance was more galling than he could bear. ''Can you find what the Bo Sin Seer might have done with her?''

''I can make discreet inquiries, but no more. The tongs of San Francisco are not like the companies of the Heavenly Kingdom. The Six Companies are known also as triads and control China with an iron grip, operating even beyond the touch of the emperor. Nothing in China is done without their knowledge and permission. Our control of San Francisco is far less sure.''

''How many tongs are there in San Francisco?''

Again Little Pete shrugged. ''Many. A few. Who can say? They form and dissolve overnight. The On Leong, Chee Kong, Suey Ying, these are powerful forces to be studied and emulated. The Bo Sin Seer is nothing more than pig manure under my heel.''

Slocum wasn't as absorbed by the ins and outs of politics in Chinatown as Little Pete. He worried about Beatrice Keller in her dusty house up on Nob Hill—and he worried about Ah So. The Chinese girl had become more than a pawn in this game. For whatever reason, powerful forces moved in San Francisco to capture her.

''I want Considine,'' Slocum said suddenly. ''If I can't find Ah So, I want Considine.''

''And Henry Keller? He, as much as his unworthy minion, is the author of your misfortune.''

''I'll see to Keller later.'' Slocum wondered how tight Little Pete was with Considine, since the man had bailed him out after Lee Chuck was arrested for murder. Had the bail money been posted on Keller's orders? For all

Slocum knew, the tong leader was as securely bound financially to Keller and Considine as the San Francisco police were.

"My men will go and make the necessary queries. It might require some small length of time to accomplish." Little Pete sat with his fingers tented, staring at Slocum as a snake might watch a bird. Slocum wondered why he was dealing with such a no-account killer; then he remembered.

He had nowhere else to turn if he wanted to find Ah So. Henry Keller, if Little Pete was to be believed, was the kingpin of crime in San Francisco, and William Considine was still his right-hand man. Even if Considine had struck out on his own, that was a falling-out between him and his boss. Slocum had a score to settle with the tall, burly man.

And the police? Keller owned them. The tongs? They served their own ends, with the Bo Sin Seer probably sure Slocum was the root of all their trouble. He had made himself extremely unpopular in San Francisco, all because he had been cheated out of his winnings at the racetrack.

"When will you know?"

"This afternoon," Little Pete said. "I will be at my usual tonsorial parlor. Meet me there." He snapped his fingers and one highbinder hanging outside the carriage reached in and handed Slocum a small business card with an address near Portsmouth Square scribbled on it. "Two o'clock," Little Pete said in his soft, sibilant voice.

As Slocum opened the carriage door to jump out, Little Pete stopped him with a long-fingered hand on his arm.

"I have no love of Henry Keller. My association has always been with Considine, and now he has outlived his usefulness."

"How do you mean?"

"A leak in my organization?" Little Pete shook his head slowly. "It cannot be any of those who have come from the Celestial Kingdom. They would not dare—and they would not have the connections required to profit by their information.''

Slocum knew Little Pete had arrived at the conclusion that Considine was the traitor in his ranks. That was fine, if he meant it. Slocum stepped from the carriage, stumbling a little as the vehicle picked up speed immediately.

He looked around and saw he was at the foot of Russian Hill with its fancy houses. Little Pete rattled on to Chinatown, leaving Slocum to his own devices. Glancing at the address on the card, he tucked it into his vest pocket and started walking. The dawn broke over the East Bay and sent long shadows ahead as he trudged his way up the streets to Nob Hill.

As he walked, Slocum kept close watch for anyone trailing him. He didn't put it past Little Pete to have someone report on his whereabouts, but he saw neither highbinders nor Considine following. Even more, the sixth sense he had come to rely on failed to report anything unusual around him.

In spite of this, Slocum took a roundabout path to reach the house where Beatrice Keller awaited him. He approached the house from the side, checked the doors and windows to be sure they were secured, and only then did he go to the front door and rap sharply.

He heard footsteps inside, the ancient wood flooring protesting even Beatrice's light tread. A dusty curtain pulled back at the side of the door and her bright emerald green eyes stared at him. She hastily opened the door. He spun in and closed and locked the door behind him.

''John, I was so worried. I ought never to have let you talk me into coming here. I've been so worried, so—''

He silenced her with a kiss. For a moment she seemed upset at this, then clung to him and buried her face into his shoulder. He felt hot tears as she silently cried.

''I made it back. That's the good news.''

''The bad is that Ah So is dead?''

''Not that bad. We attacked,'' he said, not bothering to

detail how he would have done it differently from the Gi Sin Seer, "and she had already been moved by the tong. They might have known we were on the way, or it might have been pure coincidence."

"Can you find her?"

"Little Pete is hunting now. I'm supposed to meet him this afternoon to find out what he's learned," Slocum said. His arm circled her trim body and held her close. "Don't worry. I'm not giving up. You shouldn't, either."

"It seems so awful, the things that have happened to her. To me."

"Not everything has been terrible," Slocum pointed out. He put his finger under her quaking chin and lifted her face to his. He kissed her again. This time the sparks of passion flowed in both directions. Beatrice clung to him fiercely, as if she could burn away all her uncertainty and fear in the kiss. Her body crushed against his. Through the thin fabric of her blouse and frilly undergarments, he felt the hard points of her aroused nipples poking into his chest.

He moved his hands down the sides of her sleek body, undoing a fastener here and untying a bow there. Beatrice moved sinuously against him, a snake trying to slither up a tall tree trunk. As she moved, she rubbed herself against his thigh and turned the denim wet with her outpouring of desire.

"I want you, John. Here. Now."

"In the hallway?"

"Here! Yes!"

She brooked no argument. She shivered and shucked off her clothing like a snake shedding dried skin. And Beatrice did not stop there. She unfastened his gun belt and let it drop to the wooden floor with a loud clank. Then she began working in earnest on his shirt and pants. The buttons almost popped as she got his fly open and fumbled inside for the thick stalk of his erect shaft hidden away.

Slocum caught his breath as Beatrice dropped to her knees, seized his erection, and pulled it to her mouth. Ruby lips closed on the tip, and the exquisite blond applied suction until Slocum's knees turned weak. Then she used her tongue, lashing along the underside to touch the most sensitive portions of his length, and her pearly teeth scraped and teased. As she worked with her mouth, her fingers tapped lightly on the hairy bag at the base.

Slocum reached out and laced his fingers through her silken hair, guiding her back and forth in a movement that about robbed him of his control. He felt like a young buck with his first woman.

"No more," he said, hardly trusting his voice. "You do that too good."

"I want you, John," she said, staring up at him with her bright eyes. "Please."

"There's no need to ask twice," he told her, dropping beside her on the hardwood floor. His arms circled her naked body and pulled her close. Again they kissed, tongues dashing back and forth in an erotic frolic. His hands moved ever lower on her gracefully arched back until his fingers closed on her buttocks.

He kneaded the flesh he found, trying to tear it from her body, then soothing and finally delving deeper, lower. He found a fleecy patch sopping with her inner juices hidden between her thighs.

Beatrice moaned constantly now, her arousal reaching the breaking point. She shifted her weight and pushed Slocum onto his back in the middle of the hallway. Tongue flicking out, she licked his lips and chin and neck and finally found his ear. The darting pink organ drove hard into his ear as she straddled his body.

Slocum reached between their bodies and guided himself into her intimate softness. Beatrice rose and fell once he got positioned and took his full length.

From this point on, Slocum was lost to complete desire. His hips lifted off the floor, trying to dig deeper into the woman's most private recesses. When Beatrice leaned forward and let her blond hair trail over his chest, Slocum rolled. He came out on top. Beatrice's slender legs opened wantonly for him now, and he began stroking with increasing power and penetration.

Together they went off like a Fourth of July firecracker, soaring like a rocket high into the air and gently falling back, spent. Sweaty and tired, they lay on the hardwood floor locked in one another's arms.

Face just inches from his, Beatrice said, "I hope we find Ah So, but even if we don't, it has been worth the fight, hasn't it?"

"Just knowing you is worth it," Slocum said.

Beatrice snuggled closer, rubbing herself against his body like a contented cat. Before long, Slocum found himself responding to her subtle movements, and again they made love.

Slocum had to hunt for the barbershop in spite of the address being written on the card. He found it down a one-block-long street just off Portsmouth Square. Slocum checked his watch and found he had arrived early. Impatiently pacing, he walked the length of the street and back, fuming at the delay in meeting Little Pete.

The day had passed delightfully with Beatrice Keller, but Slocum had the uneasy feeling this was the lull before the storm. He had occasionally checked out the windows to see if anyone spied on them. There had been no evidence that anyone knew Beatrice was hiding in the Nob Hill house. She had always enticed him away from the window and back to bed—or couch or kitchen table or even the floor.

He stretched, stiff and sore from his amorous activities. Mostly, he was increasingly troubled by the morass he found himself in. No matter how he turned or fought, he could not find Ah So and give Beatrice the comfort of the

Chinese girl's safety. Worse, he had not told her of her father's criminal activities, and he had no idea how she would react. Did she already suspect? Beatrice was a clever woman, and an independent one, capable of thinking for herself.

It still had to come as a shock when she found out for certain that her father's wealth came from the endeavors she worked so hard against at her Rescue Society. In a way, Slocum felt like a coward, not telling her straight out.

He opened his pocket watch cover and stared at the hands. Time moved as if it had been dipped in molasses. He closed the watch and tucked it back into his watch pocket. Slocum looked up when he heard a carriage rattling along the street. He recognized Little Pete's conveyance immediately and walked to stand in front of the barbershop entrance to wait for him.

The tong chief hopped down lightly from inside the carriage.

"Slocum, you are early. Such eagerness is a sign of impatience. You do not rush other matters, I trust?" Little Pete grinned crookedly. Slocum wanted to push his face in, but he held back. He needed the information the Gi Sin Seer leader had.

"What did you find out?" Slocum demanded.

"A shave is always a pleasure, and there are some things available in barbershops frequented by my people not offered in others. Do join me."

Slocum chafed at the delay but followed Little Pete into the barbershop. Two Chinese barbers jumped to their feet, then bowed deeply as Little Pete took the chair closest to the door. Slocum dropped into the other.

He jerked upright when the barber approached him with a tiny spoon-shaped device at the end of a long stick.

"What's that?"

"Ah," said Little Pete, enjoying Slocum's distrust. "It

cleans out earwax and permits you to hear with unexcelled clarity.''

Little Pete leaned back and let his barber use a similar contraption on him. Slocum warily kept his head immobile as the barber worked to remove earwax. He was used to getting a shave, a bath, maybe bled if the situation required it, but this was something alien to him.

''What about Ah So?'' Slocum asked when the barber dropped the wax spoon to a tray and retreated to fetch a straight razor.

''I have located the fluttering dove,'' Little Pete said. ''She will soon dampen her wings, I fear, unless we move swiftly. It is as I thought. The Bo Sin Seer have her down on the—'' Little Pete sat up in the chair and gasped.

Slocum saw the flash of knives outside. A single cut opened one of Little Pete's bodyguards' throat from ear to ear. Two flying hatchets killed the other two. Slocum struggled to reach his Colt in its cross-draw holster. The sheet spread over him got tangled and prevented an easy draw.

Three highbinders came in and spoke swiftly in sing-song Chinese. Slocum caught the words ''Bo Sin Seer'' an instant before all three used their weapons to kill Little Pete in the barber chair. Then they turned their wicked knives and hatchets in his direction.

Slocum fired from under the sheet. All he did was set fire to the sheet. He cast it off. The flaming cloth created enough confusion to keep the Bo Sin Seer highbinders away long enough for Slocum to tumble from the chair.

''He is one of Little Pete's bodyguards!'' cried the barber behind Slocum. ''Kill him!''

Slocum was torn between the lying barber and simply staying alive. A shot to the man's face would have been satisfying. Getting out the back door and racing down an alley was less satisfying but more prudent.

At the end of the alley, Slocum stopped to catch his breath—and this saved him from a hatchet swinging at eye level. He ducked, turned, and fired into the belly of a hatchet man who had circled the block, searching for his elusive would-be victim.

The highbinder grunted and fell back against the brick wall. Slocum fired a second time to keep the man from shouting to his comrades down the street.

Walking fast but trying to melt into the crush of people in Portsmouth Square proved hard, but Slocum succeeded in getting away from the Bo Sin Seer—for the time being.

18

Slocum stopped and then dived facedown into the gutter. A hail of bullets ripped through the air where he had been only a heartbeat before. Wiggling like a worm, he got to the corner and pulled himself around, using a building for temporary shelter.

He could not stay here much longer. The Bo Sin Seer had been all too eager to add his scalp to those they had claimed that afternoon. Little Pete was dead, and with the tong leader went Slocum's only chance of finding where Ah So was. But that paled into insignificance with the Bo Sin Seer highbinders after him.

He wished it were sundown so he could duck into shadow and get the hell out of San Francisco before they spotted him again. Then Slocum realized he could never do that. He had an obligation to Beatrice and to Ah So. Little Pete might no longer be able to tell where the Chinese girl was being hidden, but someone had to know. After all, Little Pete had learned of her location from someone. If only he had been given an extra minute of life so he could have passed that information along to Slocum before his murder.

The soft shuffle of Chinese slippers alerted Slocum to

approaching danger. He pressed his back against the cold brick wall and waited. A hunched over Chinese came into view. At first, Slocum thought it was an old man making his way along painfully. Then he saw the wicked gleam of the long, slender-bladed knife in the Celestial's hand.

Swinging his Colt Navy, he caught the man in the temple and sent him crashing to the ground. Slocum kicked the knife away and rapidly searched his fallen stalker. All he found was a second razor-sharp knife hidden in a sheath under the quilted jacket.

The longer he stayed out where the tong could find him, the better the chance he would end up like Little Pete. But Slocum's problem was about the same as the missing Ah So's. He had no one to turn to for help.

Getting to the docks gave him a measure of concealment. Although it was hours from sundown, the sailors were already working at getting stinking drunk. More than this, many of the ships prepared to leave on the evening tide. Last-minute cargo went into holds and seamen bid a fond farewell to dry land for another few months.

When he reached Meiggs's Pier with its Cobweb Palace at the far end, Slocum cut toward the center of the Barbary Coast. Few Chinese ventured here, and those who did walked in fear of their lives. Too many of the residents considered them fair game for any vile notion that came into their whiskey-besotted brains.

Slocum trudged uphill to Beatrice's house and worked his way to the rear, certain the Bo Sin Seer killers had not trailed him. From their aggressive methods, he thought they would have shot or stabbed him on sight, but he could not risk Beatrice's life. The highbinders might have followed him with an eye toward taking her prisoner again. Too many factors entered this deadly race against time.

He sat heavily on the back porch, thinking what to do. Getting Beatrice out of San Francisco seemed the most sensible. To hell with Ah So.

"Ah So," he muttered. Something worked deep in his brain, tickling here and prodding there. Little Pete had not told him where the Chinese girl was being hidden, but he had hinted at it, thinking to tantalize with his vague references.

"John, you're back so soon!"

"What?" He jerked around, hand going for his six-shooter at Beatrice's words. "I've been gone forever."

"Oh, no," she said. "You've been gone only about an hour. At least, it's only three o'clock."

Slocum hardly believed her until he checked his watch. She was right. It seemed as if he had spent an eternity dodging the tong hatchet men when it had been less than an hour.

"What did you learn?" Beatrice sat beside him. He wanted to push her back inside but decided it hardly mattered. He would sneak her from the city and that would end her danger. But that tiny seed within his head began to sprout.

"Little Pete's dead," Slocum said. Beatrice gasped, but he went on, not wanting to go into detail about the tong leader's death. "He hinted where Ah So might be. If only I could put it all together. I have the feeling time is against us, unless I can get a hold of it."

"What did he say?"

"Nothing definite. He was always vague, as if he tormented me with the truth, dancing around it without actually saying anything."

"I see," Beatrice said thoughtfully. "I—"

"What did you say?" Slocum sat up straight and looked at her. Everything fell into place for him with a single word.

"I was just saying that I understand what he was doing. A man who lives by blackmail must always hint and pretend to know more than he really does."

"Sea," Slocum said. "The Bo Sin Seer is going to ship Ah So back to China."

"When?" Beatrice's eyes went wide in fear that the girl would be forever lost.

"Tonight. At eventide there must be a ship sailing for the Orient." Slocum's mind raced. Several would be setting sail. He remembered his race along the docks and the furor of activity as any number of the sailing ships prepared for voyages. How many headed to China and how could he find the one where Ah So was held captive? As if she were being shanghaied, she would be kept below decks until the ship was far out to sea.

Slocum realized how lucky he had been escaping Captain Craig's ship. A cold hatred of William Considine built in him again, as he remembered how he had ended up aboard that ship. Sold.

Ah So must feel the same—except she was being returned to China for stealing the emperor's pearls. That had to be the reason the Bo Sin Seer was so eager to get her back to their homeland. A huge reward might be offered for the return of a thief of such note. But what of the pearls Ah So had taken?

"I've got to find her," Slocum said. "There can't be more than a handful of ships sailing for China."

"I can ask Papa to find out," Beatrice said.

"No!" Slocum replied too sharply. She looked at him. He knew he had to think up some excuse or tell her what Little Pete had claimed. That might be a lie, but in his gut, Slocum knew the tong blackmailer had spoken the truth. "You don't want to do that. Considine," he said, mind fumbling for the right excuse. "He might be waiting for you to try to reach your father."

"But I ought to let Papa know I am all right. He must think I am dead. Or worse." She shivered and rubbed her hands up and down her legs, as if trying to cleanse them of unseen filth.

"I want you to stay here," Slocum said. "I don't want to have to worry about rescuing you, too. And more important, you have to be here when I get back with Ah So.

You speak her lingo and I don't. She'll need comforting.''

"I speak Chinese a little," Beatrice said reluctantly. "I see your point. She will need great reassurance to keep from being terribly frightened."

"You're right," Slocum said, letting the woman make her own arguments better than he ever could. "I've got to get down to the Embarcadero right away. Finding that ship's not going to be easy."

"But the tong killers," Beatrice protested.

"I'll keep out of their way," he said, realizing when Beatrice mentioned the Bo Sin Seer that he was going to be walking into the center of their power. Every hatchet man in their bloodthirsty tong was likely to be guarding Ah So until she set sail.

He kissed Beatrice, wished he could linger, then retraced his tracks all the way down to the bay.

"Them furrin devils?" snarled the old salt. "They's all over the place. Filthy barstids."

"You know what they calls us?" chimed in another sailor, half the other's age but still weathered and missing most of his teeth. "*Kwan fei* they calls us. Foreign devils. Us foreign!" He spat between the gap formed by missing front teeth.

"A ship's set to sail for China tonight," Slocum said, "and the tong hatchet men will be all around it, like they're guarding something important. Which ship might that be?" Slocum looked from one seaman to the other. The two exchanged glances, and the older one wiped his lips before speaking.

"Hate to say anythin' contrary 'bout a good man, but Cap'n Nick Cameron's known for carryin' contraband."

"Not that there's anythin' wrong with that," cut in the younger sailor. "No one's fault there are so many screwy laws keepin' decent men from makin' a livin'."

"This might be a slave he's carrying," Slocum said.

"Don't hold with that. Never cottoned much to them Yankees, but keepin' someone in chains ain't no way to live."

"Which is Cameron's ship?"

"The *Petaluma*, down on Pier Fourteen. Named for a town up north, where he hails from."

Slocum thanked the pair and moved down the Embarcadero, counting slips and piers until he saw four highbinders lounging about, trying not to be too conspicuous but standing out as if they had been painted bright orange. Amid the Chinese moving barges and loading cargo, only these four lounged back, watching every move along the pier.

Slocum spent the better part of an hour watching preparations for the China clipper's departure. As he watched, he grew increasingly edgy. The Bo Sin Seer killers never strayed far, and when they did, no fewer than two remained to watch who walked out the pier the dozen paces to the gangplank. At times, as many as a dozen patrolled the wharf.

Ah So had to be aboard the *Petaluma*, but rescuing her would be a chore for an army.

Slocum had only his trusty Colt Navy and his wits to serve him.

When it became apparent the Bo Sin Seer highbinders would not leave until after the ship sailed, Slocum knew he had to act. Going into a shed, he found an old broom and a tar pot. He spent ten minutes getting a fire started to melt the tar and another five dipping the thick tar on the broom. It took only an instant to set the sticky mess afire.

With the broom crackling and sending sparks everywhere, Slocum left the shed and calmly walked toward the *Petaluma*. When he got within tossing distance, he spun the broom around and around and let it fly. For a second, none of the highbinders noticed what he was doing. Then they all reacted.

"Fire!" Slocum shouted. "Fire! Call the firemen!"

He drew and fired three quick rounds into the midst of the highbinders, scattering them. By now the broom had stuck to the side of the ship and merrily burned just above the water line. Some sailors jumped overboard in an attempt to reach it and pull it free. Others shouted contradictory orders. The confusion grew into outright panic.

Still, Slocum wasn't aboard the ship. He swung down under the edge of the dock and let a few of the highbinders rush past. Only then did he try to get aboard. He had to use his three remaining rounds on tong killers intent on preventing anyone's entry onto the ship.

"We're sinking!" he cried. "We're on fire! Abandon ship!" He went the length of the deck shouting his orders. The smoke rising from the ship's stern gave credence to his claims. The chaos he had created on the dock added to the fear crashing through the *Petaluma* like a tidal wave.

Slocum ducked down a hatch and dropped into the hold. It took him a few minutes to get his bearings, but when he did, he found the captain's quarters quickly enough.

He took time to reload, then shot off the lock on the door to the captain's quarters. He kicked in the door and found Ah So sitting on the narrow bunk, her face pale and her eyes wide with fear.

"We're getting out of here!" Slocum shouted at her. The girl shied away like a skittish pony. He rushed to her side and grabbed her arm to shake some sense into her.

She started to point behind them. Slocum pushed Ah So in one direction and dived the opposite in time to avoid getting a knife in the back. He started shooting and killed the highbinder trying to prevent the escape. Scrambling to his feet, Slocum got off two more rounds into the narrow corridor outside the captain's room. Then he slammed the door.

"Move that trunk," he called to Ah So. "Block the door!"

She obeyed. Whether she understood him or simply realized it was the only way they were going to stay alive another few seconds, Slocum did not know. The heavy sea chest blocked the door. For a few seconds. From the thunder of feet outside, every tong assassin in San Francisco was outside, trying to get in.

Slocum lifted his Colt and knew it wouldn't do him any good. He might have one or two rounds left. No more. And he sure as hell couldn't fight his way through so many of the enraged Bo Sin Seer hatchet men.

He found himself standing in the center of the room, his arm around Ah So's shoulders as if he could protect her from the perils of the world. Slocum wondered what would protect him.

19

Slocum didn't bother to take the time to reload. If he had, both he and Ah So would have been dead. The highbinders worked furiously to hack away the heavy door using their hatchets. Slocum grabbed the girl by the arm and pulled her toward a small window set high on the back wall of the cabin. Jumping to a table, he dragged her behind like a balky mule. She struggled, and Slocum did not know why. Better to dive overboard than to be caught by the tong assassins.

"No!" she cried. Slocum ignored her as he battered out the window with the butt of his six-shooter. He hoisted the protesting Chinese girl up and shoved her through the window as the highbinders broke down the door. A quick shot in their direction drove them back. This was all it took for Slocum to follow Ah So through the tiny window and into the icy water of San Francisco Bay.

He sputtered and kicked to get away from the *Petaluma* before the hatchet men decided to follow. A flailing arm struck him. Slocum rolled in the water and saw Ah So could not swim. He grabbed her around the shoulders and got her floating on her back before he started kicking powerfully to put as much distance between them and the ship as he could.

"We're away but we're not free," he told her as they swam. He didn't know how much English she understood, but it had to be more than he knew of her language.

They reached the docks and the ragged, barnacle-encrusted wood supports gave Slocum a chance to rest by hanging on rather than swimming. Ah So floundered a bit then hugged one pillar for dear life. Above, Slocum heard the thunder of running feet. The escape had stirred the tong killers like boiling water poured down an anthill.

"That way," Slocum told the girl, pointing toward the end of the dock. He feared they would be discovered at any instant. If so, having dry land under his feet would give a better chance for escape than trying to swim with a girl who sank better than she swam.

Ah So hesitantly made her way in that direction, lurching and splashing noisily from one pillar to the next until they reached the muddy end of the pier. From the sibilant conversation over his head, Slocum knew the place was alive with Bo Sin Seer killers. Avoiding them would be a problem. Or would it?

From above came the aggrieved, "Whatya mean there's no fire? I can smell smoke."

"No fire. All out."

"I want to check for myself. Somebody reported a fire, and I ain't lettin' the entire wharf go up like it did a couple years ago. The whole danged place is a fire hazard."

"No fire. All out," repeated the highbinder, but the protest fell on deaf ears.

"Come on, men. Look sharp, now, and be sure there's not even a spark still warm out here." The firemen trooped along the pier. Slocum pulled at Ah So's sleeve and got her moving. In the confusion of the firemen investigating the small blaze he had set, Slocum knew he and Ah So could slip away.

They ducked behind a fire engine, got barked at by the Dalmatian standing patient guard in the high seat, then made their way from the docks and into San Francisco. Only when they had put a dozen blocks between them and the *Petaluma* did Slocum breathe a little easier. What was he to do now?

"We've got to get you to Miss Keller," he said. The expression on the girl's face told him he had said the right words. Mention of Beatrice Keller put everything right with the Chinese girl. She followed obediently now, shadowing Slocum's every move as he made his way across town and up the winding streets near Nob Hill.

Slocum felt the need to go to ground fast, but he feared the highbinders might have followed them. He waited five minutes outside the house where Beatrice Keller ought to be, worrying that he saw no sign of her inside. Still, he saw no hint that the tong hatchet men had followed, either. Beatrice might be laying low and waiting for him to return with Ah So.

"We're going straight into the house," he told the girl. "No bowing and scraping. Just go right on in." He shoved her in front of him, but she stopped and he saw she would not walk in front of him. Incongruously, he noticed how incredibly small her feet were; they had been bound until she was almost crippled, yet she had not made a peep of protest as he had hurried her through the streets.

Slocum shook his head. This was too much for him to take. Getting Ah So into Beatrice's capable hands couldn't happen too soon.

He took the front steps two at a time and reached the porch. The front door was open, but the interior of the house was unlit. Slocum got an uneasy feeling until he saw a note on the table by the door.

A quick scan of it assured him Beatrice was all right. "She's gone to fetch a carriage for the two of you," he said. "You can get out of town. Oakland, somewhere."

It hardly mattered to him anymore. Slocum felt an incredible tiredness washing over him like the waves from an ocean of lethargy. He turned to tell Ah So to get something to eat for the both of them when he saw a moving shadow. Slocum's hand went for his six-gun but he froze when a cruel laugh echoed through the house.

"You're one hell of a hard man to find, Slocum. You been stickin' your nose where it don't belong. You tried to plug me, then you got Little Pete killed, but not before you told him I sold him out."

"Didn't you?" Slocum asked William Considine.

"Of course I did. I sold out Keller, too, the fat son of a bitch. I know what he takes in. I wanted a bigger cut, and he wouldn't give it to me. So I took what was mine."

"You were playing all sides against each other," Slocum said. Considine had his arm around Ah So's throat, holding her tight. In his right hand rested a six-shooter, pointed squarely at Slocum.

"I worked with Little Pete to fix the races, I cut in on Keller's opium smuggling, I sold them both out to the Bo Sin Seer in exchange for running the two whorehouses. Then that yellow monkey Little Pete burned both of them to ground. It was only pure luck I chanced to see you and the little pearl here runnin' from the docks."

Considine did not expect any trouble from Ah So. He yelped in surprise as much as pain when she bit him hard on his forearm. In that brief instant of distraction, his six-gun wavered from the middle of Slocum's head.

Slocum's hand flashed to his Colt. He drew and fired. The hammer fell on a wet percussion cap. Never hesitating, Slocum launched himself and felt a hot streak along his back as Considine fired. Slocum's shoulder drove hard into Ah So's belly, but the impact carried all three of them out of the house and onto the porch. Considine fought to keep his feet under him. He missed when he passed the top step.

Slocum rolled and pushed Ah So to one side. He scrambled to his feet and lunged to land hard atop Considine.

The man's pistol went off again, and again the bullet missed its mark. Slocum hit Considine as hard as he could, sending a jolt all the way up his to his shoulder.

"Have to do better than that," the huge man said, shaking his head and batting Slocum away like an annoying, buzzing insect. Slocum tumbled back and fell heavily. Considine retrieved his gun and took careful aim.

A wet pop sounded and Considine grabbed for his neck. Ah So had retrieved Slocum's fallen six-shooter and tried to shoot Considine. The next round misfired, too, but it sent a bullet tumbling out the barrel to nick him on the neck. This distraction proved fatal to Considine, not from the bullet fired by Ah So but from Slocum's determination. Slocum wrenched Considine's six-gun from his hand and fired point-blank.

Considine's eyes went wide, he clutched at his chest and the spreading red wetness there, then he sank to his knees. From there he fell to one side, dead.

Slocum stared at the fallen giant and wondered at his lack of emotion. He had hated the man for all he had done. Now there was . . . nothing.

"You are a dangerous man, Slocum," came a voice he recognized all too well. "Don't turn around or I will cut you down where you stand."

"Looking for your right-hand man, Keller?"

"Actually, no. I was hunting for you and this Chinese bitch." Ah So squealed. Slocum chanced a look over his shoulder and saw Henry Keller with his foot in the middle of the girl's back, pinning her to the porch. "I never knew Beatrice had this house. She is a surprisingly capable young woman. Like her mother, damn her eyes!"

"What now?"

"I could not find Beatrice, so I assume you sent her away. That is all right. She will believe anything I tell her if you and this meddling Chinee aren't around to contradict me."

"She doesn't know anything about your illegal dealings," Slocum said.

"Illegal? A few laws might be bent a trifle, but everything I do is legal. Or ought to be. The opium dens, for instance. And the brothels. Perhaps you're referring to my other small sources of income?"

Slocum's finger tightened on the trigger as he started to turn and fire.

"Drop the gun, Slocum. If you move so much as one muscle, I'll shoot you in the back where you stand," Keller warned. From the cold tone, Slocum knew the man meant it.

"What now?" Slocum said, putting the six-shooter down on the ground. "What are you planning to do with Ah So and me?"

"Kill you. I can't have witnesses to my indiscreet behavior. I have a social position to maintain."

"The girl knows nothing. She's only a pawn being moved around. Let her go. She doesn't even speak English."

"How noble of you, Slocum. You are quite right about her, though," Keller said, his tone changing. "She is incredibly valuable to the right people. She is the emperor's concubine, all run off to find a new life in this fine land."

"What's that?" demanded Slocum. "She stole pearls from the emperor."

"Stole pearls? Hardly. She is called the Emperor's Radiant Pearl because of her incredible beauty. The tong will pay a fortune to get her back and return her to their emperor to gain favor. It is little enough payment for my troubles. Thanks for reminding me there was a buck to be made off her. But you, Slocum, I fear you must die to tie up loose ends."

A carriage rattled along the lane leading to the house. Slocum saw the driver and started to cry out to her.

"Beatrice!" muttered Keller, making his daughter's name sound like a curse. "I might have to remove her, also. Too many loose ends, too many tongues wagging. She always had a knack for being at the wrong place at the wrong time.''

Slocum dropped to one knee and went for the gun, but strange whooshing sounds filled the air. By the time he hit the ground, grabbed the six-shooter, and got to a position where he could fire, he saw Henry Keller tottering with two knives in his belly. As the man's knees gave out and he twisted slowly, a hatchet became apparent.

Which had killed him, Slocum didn't know. The high-binders had found them finally. He got off two quick shots at one hatchet man dressed in his dark quilted jacket as three more moved in on Ah So.

"Run!" Slocum yelled to the girl. Ah So obeyed as fast as her tiny feet could take her. Slocum pushed her past him in the direction of the carriage.

"Ah So! Get in," ordered Beatrice.

"Get out of here. I'll hold them off," Slocum said.

"No, John, it's your death!" Beatrice started to bring the carriage around. He waved her off. "John," Beatrice Keller said plaintively.

"Get out of here. Save yourself and Ah So. Your pa's dead. The highbinders killed him. Now drive!"

He fired again and realized he was running out of time. How many rounds remained in Considine's six-shooter? Slocum couldn't remember. He snatched up his fallen Colt and shoved it into his holster, intending to reload it later, when there was time.

"John, thank you. Thank you!" With those parting words, Beatrice whipped the horses and the carriage lurched away. Slocum had done all he could to protect her. She might never find out that her father's fortune came from every illegal venture imaginable in a wide-open town like San Francisco. Or she might, but she would be safe then, she and her Chinese ward.

He emptied Considine's six-gun and took refuge behind the dead man's body. He fumbled in Considine's coat pockets and found spare ammo. Slocum reloaded one round in time to fire into a highbinder running on silent feet from the house. The slug hit the man high in the shoulder and spun him around. He fell, cursing loudly in Chinese. This gave Slocum a few extra seconds to reload completely.

His fingers closed on Considine's thick wallet. He took it, stuffing it into his own pocket. The greenbacks there might provide enough to get him out of town—if he got away alive. He began a measured fire as he had so many times during the war when the Yankees tried to overrun his position.

The slow, steady fire and hitting every target drove the highbinders back to the shelter of the house to regroup.

"What's going on? We got the police on the way!" cried a neighbor from down the street. "You damned yellow bastards can't go killin' people up here. Take your wars back to Chinatown!"

The hatchet men understood enough of the shouted curse to pull back a little more. Slocum emptied Considine's six-gun again in their direction, and this time he lit out running. He passed a patrol of specials huffing and puffing their way up the hill to maintain order.

He knew the highbinders would not fight the policemen. They were away from familiar territory, without support. A volley sounded, followed by loud shouts and running feet. Slocum slowed his own retreat and walked more purposefully. He tossed away Considine's gun and checked the man's wallet. A thick wad of scrip, maybe a thousand dollars, provided some small pay for all he had been through.

Slocum considered tracking down Beatrice Keller, then decided to let the gorgeous blonde follow her own path. It certainly wasn't his.

Where did his path lead? Slocum wasn't sure, but it might be east, across the Sierra Nevadas and into the Comstock. He could always find a miner or two who didn't know the odds at the poker table. Or he could head north to Oregon. Pretty country up north and always needing hands good with horses.

John Slocum didn't know where he was headed, but he knew one thing. He wasn't staying in San Francisco with its tong killers one instant longer than necessary.

JAKE LOGAN

TODAY'S HOTTEST ACTION WESTERN!